Thomas Emory van Bebber

The Flight into Egypt

Thomas Emory van Bebber

The Flight into Egypt

ISBN/EAN: 9783744712019

Printed in Europe, USA, Canada, Australia, Japan

Cover: Foto ©Andreas Hilbeck / pixelio.de

More available books at **www.hansebooks.com**

DEDICATION

TO

W. C. VAN BIBBER, M. D.,

OF BALTIMORE.

————

Permit me to dedicate these Poems to one who, notwithstanding a slight difference in our way of spelling the family name, has always been to me the truest of brothers, both by ties of blood, and by never-ceasing acts of fraternal affection. Frequent researches among old family letters and records, some of these extending in point of time as far back as two centuries, and in point of space to the ancient city of Utrecht, in Holland, have induced me to use an *e* instead of an *i* in the second syllable of our common name. This trifle would be unworthy of mention, were it not that it might cause surprise and misapprehension in the minds of some not acquainted with the circumstances.

Should the Poems, and particularly the principal one, entitled "The Flight into Egypt," secure to the writer as high a reputation in literature as you, my brother, have so deservedly won for yourself in your profession, he would deem himself fortunate, and might hope that some mutual friend might honor us with the applausive Latin quotation, "*Par nobile Fratrum.*" But should failure, instead of success, await my efforts, this Dedication will remain as a proof of affection on my part, without detracting in the least from the honor of your well-merited laurels.

SANTA BARBARA, August 15, 1880.

CONTENTS.

MINOR POEMS.

THE FLIGHT INTO EGYPT.

BOOK I.

HOLYLAND.

BOOK II.

BORDERLAND.

BOOK III.

BORDERLAND CONTINUED.

MINOR POEMS.

SANGUINARIA.

Deep in the woods, midst oak leaves dry and sere,
    Midst moss and prickly burrs,
    Where the lone ring-dove chirrs,
Or where, aroused by random footstep near,
    The startled peasant whirrs

In leveled flight along the fern-clad brooks,
    A wild-flower may be found,
    Scarce peeping from the ground,
About the time of Easter.   In moist nooks,
    With solitude around,

And cloistered from its birth, it shrinks from sight.
    Ring, from yon sacred pile,
    Sweet Easter-bells, the while
To count its folded petals, ermine-white,
    We tread some forest aisle.

Eight flower-leaves? Eight? Without a spot or stripe?
  Oh! how our hearts should pant
  O'er this pure woodland plant,
When in it we behold a flowery type
  Of the New Covenant—

Of a new Sabbath. Should you pierce its side
  With cruel murderous knife,
  Large purple drops of life
Ooze from the wound, as erst from His who died
  To quell sin's serpent strife.

But more to fill our spirits with amaze,
  Pure plant of modest mien!
  A leaf of tender green,
Cleft in seven parts, type of the seven first days,
  Clasping thy stalk is seen.

Thus springing spotless from the damps of death,
  Self-shrinking, thou dost pray;
  Nor can the star of day
Impart aroma to thy scentless breath,
  Or give thee colors gay.

So much the more, cold flower, dost thou dispense
  An incorporeal heat,
  Drawn from no solar seat,
But thrilling rapturous through the *inner* sense
  Like angel-kisses sweet.

THE BOW OF CALYCANTHUS.

It was a mild Sabbath afternoon, in the early part of February, that a father and his three children strolled forth to bask in the sun beneath the southern side of a high garden wall. Not a spring bird had yet made its appearance; not a violet or heart's-ease had opened its petals; the wheat fields as yet showed no tint of returning greenness, and yet the temperature of the air in that sheltered spot was delicious. The youngest of the three children, a boy of five, had, in passing, plucked from a *shrub bush* a bough, from which he had fashioned for himself both bow and arrows. This plant, as is well known, retains the fragrance of its bark all through the winter, and may, with propriety, be termed an *ever-sweet*. One of its names is "Carolina Allspice," another the simple word "shrub," perhaps from the fact that of all shrubs it is the most interesting, whilst in botanical works it is called by the high-sounding title of Calycanthus. As the father viewed his boy thus equipped, he could not forbear calling to mind the image of Camdeo or Camadeva, the Cupid of India, who is represented as "armed with a bow of sugar-cane, with a string of beads, and five arrows, each pointed with an Indian blossom." The moon—and what is more delicately beautiful than the moon of daylight?—hung like a floating lump of ice near the zenith. Under such circumstances, the father, we may suppose, *might* have composed something better than the following poetical trifle; but as it is the best he seems capable of, it is submitted as received from his own hands.

My plaided boy-archer is bending his bow;
   In bright tartans prankt, from his clan thus
Some Highland lad starts on the chase of the roe;
   No violet yet blooms, no gay polyanthus,
And yet the light zephyrs that round the boy blow
   Are scented with sweet Calycanthus.

The heavens, this bright sunny-clear afternoon,
   Seem enwreathed with supreme amaranthus;
Sky, water, and earth are all dancing in tune,
   And as joy's brimming chalice, high-hung, has o'er-
     ran thus,
The rosy boy shoots at the dimly-seen moon
   With spiced arrows of sweet Calycanthus.

As the shaft he draws back with a Cupid-like hand,
  And points it at heaven's blue dome, a
Fragrance of bruises around him is fanned;
  Oh! had the bough ripened, some maid had borne
    home a
Full bosom of odors more mellow and bland,
  Blood-warm with a richer aroma.

But why with regrets need we darken the joy
  That sweetens life's lessening span thus,
And why should the sport which so gladdens the boy
  Not gladden as well the grown man? Thus,
"On with your archery," cry we, " my boy,
  One bough from the bush will by no means destroy
    All the shrubs of our sweet Calycanthus."

SONNET ON A BEETLE PICKED UP ON THE SEASHORE.

How short our longest fathom-lines can reach
  When sounding secret Nature's mystic law!
  Walking where ever-booming billows draw
Their varying surf-lines on the fluted beach,
Intent to learn what Ocean old might teach,
  I saw and heard what thrilled me with pleased awe.
  A text in unknown characters I saw,
On which a sage, before the flood, might preach
  Deep sermons, and inculcate line on line.
The text was couched in characters antique,
  Such as might fit some immemorial shrine
That had seemed ancient to an ancient Greek;
Three letters on each wing! Oh! could they speak,
  Be sure they would proclaim some truth divine.

AWAKENING OF THE BREEZE IN SUMMER.

How calm this summer morn reposes!
How dreamily each tree-top dozes!
    Softly creep
    Slumbers deep
O'er poppy-heads and beds of pillowed roses.

Untwinkling gems hang, scarce adorning
    The dead-still trees;
The flowers, top-heavy, seem their dewdrops scorning;
    Wake, gentle breeze!
Awake! and rouse to life this drowsy morning.

It wakes! The floweret from its pillow
    Heaves with delight;
    All shivering, white
With joy, upleaps the maple and the weeping willow.

Arch aspens, which have been dissembling
    An ill-feigned sleep,
    With lightning-leap
Now thrill and flutter into rapturous trembling.

O'er wheat fields which have stood all moveless, sunning
    Their gold-green heads,
    Now, rapid spreads
Circle on circle, up the high hills running.

Words can not paint how much thy advent blesses,
    Thou breezelet sweet,
    Fanning flushed summer's heat,
And sporting with my loved one's raven tresses.

WINTER POEMS.

I.

A BRIGHT MORNING.

Now beneath unclouded skies
  Snowy fields are all ablaze,
Now the whizzing snowball flies,
  While the school-boy as he plays
Often shields his dazzled eyes;
  Hark! the many-colored sleighs,
Flying rainbows hung with bells,
How their music sinks and swells!

Angels float on sunny cars
  Through the heavenly mansions bright;
Too much radiance only mars
  Mortal man's unquickened sight;
Let us wait until the stars
  And the moon adorn the night,
Then with merriest bells let's go,
Lovely lady, o'er the snow.

II.

ICE-PICTURES.

Lo! where the freezing waters slumber
  Deep in the bosom of yon wood,
Bright fairy castles without number
  Gleam gayly o'er the pictured flood;
Here, crystal warriors slowly marching
  Tread up and down the turrets tall,
There, deer with antlers overarching,
  Repose beneath the castle-wall.

Here, fleetly ranging o'er blue mountains,
　Trim hunters rouse the jolly morn,
There, knights are grouped around the fountains,
　Each with his spear and silver horn.
Behold yon forests wildly gleaming,
　O'erhung with pearls of countless price!
Say, can the quiet waters, dreaming,
　Imprint their visions thus on ice?

And can not summer's sunshine render
　The waves as fair as when they freeze,
Though then they mirror back the splendor
　Of golden clouds and hanging trees;
Though o'er them then the red-bird glances
　And throws his image down below,
And many a crimson flow'ret dances
　Beside the waters as they flow?

The slavish mirror blindly molding
　The shadowy shapes of real things,
Is now an active power unfolding
　Its own self-formed imaginings;
And where in summer leaves were waving
　Far down its depths on headlong trees,
Now the fair stream is seen engraving
　Its own delicious phantasies.

Then we beheld wild-clustering roses
　Adown its bosom growing ripe,
But now that magic glass discloses
　Strange flowers without a prototype.
Thus, when o'er fields of desolation,
　Hope's withered leaves and blooms are whirled,
Fresh thoughts spring forth by self-creation,
　And, freezing, form a brighter world.

III.

ON SEEING THE MOON RISE BEHIND A DISTANT WOOD.

As when some stately man-of-war,
Slow rocking near the harbor bar,
Is seen by sunrise from afar
With every tiny rope and spar
    Athwart the red clouds heaving;
Thus, o'er yon hill-top's rocky brow
Which darkening veils o'erhung till now,
Each little twig, each slender bough
    Is seen its network weaving.

More charming than the woods of June,
Like stones for Gothic churches hewn,
Strange lines are penciled on the moon;
But soon the fairy show, too soon,
    Departs, and leaves no traces;
The trees, like things deformed and black,
Sink to their former darkness back,
While she pursues her upward track
    With all the lunar graces.

THE VESTAL VIRGIN OF TIBUR (THE MODERN TIVOLI).

Where classic Arno's billows roar
    Adown the toppling Appenine,
A temple stood in days of yore
    Engirt with cypress trees and pine;
High-poised above the cascade's foam,
    The view extended many a mile,
And on clear days the towers of Rome
    Were seen from off the peristyle.

The vapors of the waterfall
Full oft around its columns curled;
Bent in a circle was its wall,
Type of the universal world;*
Along its sculptured frieze was seen
A yoke of oxen moving slow,
As if in search of pastures green,
Or meads where golden willows grow.

There, many a year, sweet vestal maid,
Far from thy friends and pleasant home
Thou trod'st the circling colonnade,
Or knelt beneath the sphery dome;
Methinks I see thee even now!
Around thy head waves many a tress,
A saintly halo decks thy brow,
And thou art steeped in loveliness.

And thou so long hast gazed upon
The flame that burns on Vesta's shrine,
The hallowed essence of the sun,
That unpolluted thoughts are thine,
And thou art purer than the moon.
The sun-fire is thy paramour,
And like a statue freshly hewn,
Thou art all heavenly, white and pure.

*The circular form always observable in the temples of Vesta has been variously accounted for by different authors. Dion. Hal. thought it was intended to represent the Earth. Plutarch, however, gives a far more beautiful and philosophical explanation. He remarks that " Numa built the temple of Vesta, where the perpetual fire was to be kept, in an *orbicular form;* not intending to represent the figure of the Earth, as if that were meant by Vesta; but the frame of the Universe, in the center of which the Pythagoreans place the element of fire, and give it the names of Vesta and Unity. The Earth they suppose not to be without motion, nor situated in the center of the world, but to make its revolution round the sphere of fire, being one neither of the most valuable nor principal parts of the great machine."—See Life of Numa, 169.

IDUNA'S APPLES.

———

THE following little poem is founded on a circumstance mentioned in the Icelandic Edda, the Pantheon of Scandinavian Mythology. The gods prevented the effect of old age and decay, by eating certain apples, trusted to the care of Iduna, the goddess of perpetual youth. Once on a time, Lok, the Momus of the Scandinavians, craftily conveyed her away, together with her invaluable fruit, and concealed her in a wood, under the custody of a giant. What happened after this disastrous event, forms the subject of these verses. For those who have never investigated the idle but somewhat curious system of mythical belief, adopted by the northern nations of Europe prior to the introduction of Christianity, it may be well to state a few of its leading and most prominent peculiarities. Braga was the god of poetry, eloquence, and wisdom; he corresponds with the Apollo of the Greeks and Romans. The Rainbow (*Bifrost*) was the bridge, communicating from heaven to earth. Its extremities were watched over by *Hiemdaller*, a god who slept lighter than the birds, and whose sense of hearing was so acute, that he could perceive the sound made by the growing of grass in the fields, and wool on the backs of sheep; he held in one hand a sword, and in the other a trumpet, the noise of which was heard through all worlds. *Niord* was the Neptune of the North. *Thialfe* was so remarkable for his skill in skating, that he is reported to have outstripped the ghost of a giant. Upon the whole, it may be remarked that this mythology, along with much that is ridiculous and extravagant, contains many things both highly philosophical and strikingly poetical.

I.

Long years had passed since Lok had stolen away
   The fruit which could the bloom of youth recall;
The gods and heroes all were growing gray;
   Loud lamentations filled Valhalla's hall;
   And though the shields, high hanging from the wall,
Still from their burnished orbs shed dazzling light,
   Yet now no more to herald's joyous call
Upsprang mailed warriors clad in armor bright,
To spur the bounding steed, or rush to frantic fight.

II.

Year after year they all grew more aghast,
　For still the rosy apples were not found,
When Braga, god of poesy, at last
　Struck from his rusty harp a feeble sound,
　And tottered forth upon the mission bound,
Swearing to find them, or return no more.
　And now the gods are all assembled round,
　Yet, oh! how different from the days of yore;
In gloomy groups they stand, and eye the golden door.

III.

They form, I trow, a melancholy scene!
　One stays his tottering members with a staff,
And where the smile of triumph once had been.
　Now dwells fatuity with idiot laugh;
　Another grasps the bowl, and strives to quaff
Forgetfulness of age and racking pain;
　But, lo! it tumbles from his hand, ere half
The waves of liquid poison he can drain,
And on the flooded floor the dotard drops amain.

IV.

No more does Thor against the giants march,
　Inglorious rests his mallet by his side;
No more along the rainbow's watery arch
　On prancing steed can haut Hiemdaller ride,
　Or blow his trump erst echoing far and wide;
Niord's dominion o'er the waves is quelled,
　He now no more can govern ocean's tide;
E'en Odin's potent fingers, which upheld
The scepter of the gods, now shake with palsied eld.

V.

Thialfe against a fluted column stands,
    And idly of his former triumph prates,
And often sighs, and often wrings his hands,
    And often gazes on his rusty skates;
    Aye, as Iduna's advent he awaits,
He calls to mind the days of youth, when he
    On circling steel, through morning's rosy gates,
Before careering winds did often flee,
Swifter than lightning's flash, across the frozen sea.

VI.

Oh! who can tell how sad and slow the time
    Rolls o'er those blasted forms assembled there!
What now can Verse, what now can Runic rhyme,
    To ease their pain, or soothe their deep despair!
    With squalid beard, sunk jaw, and unkempt hair,
One, like a maniac, stares with vacant eye;
    Another beats with shrunken arm the air,
Or vainly wishes for the power to die,
Or tunes with piping voice a feeble battle-cry.

VII.

The most, in sullen torpor crouching, stirred
    Nor hand nor foot, o'erspread with pallid hue,
When lo! the sound of distant harp was heard,
    Which ever louder, clearer, merrier grew,
    And they beheld—oh! glorious sight in sooth—
Fair Braga and Iduna. Swift she threw
The apples on the floor—with greedy tooth
They seize—eat—clash their shields—O God, the joys of
        Youth!

VIII.

Instant through all the hall are seen to wax
  A thousand glorious forms; echoes the hymn
Of triumph—lance, spear, falchion, battle-ax,
  Flash lightning-like—heroic eyes, erst dim,
  Resume their ancient luster—to the brim
They fill the bowl, whence maddening joy is quaft—
  Upsprings the dance—in mazy cirques they swim
Around each column tall and fluted shaft,
Swift as revolving leaves, which rushing whirlwinds waft.

IX.

And when the first mad burst of joy began
  A somewhat milder aspect to assume,
A band of female figures, warped and wan,
  Who heretofore had lain in torpid gloom,
  Inanimate as corpses in a tomb,
Now round Iduna kneel in pallid ring.
  Anon, they taste the immortal fruit—fresh bloom
Spreads o'er their cheeks—like new-fledged birds in
    spring,
All rosy red they mount, and soar on buoyant wing.

X.

At last, to crown the glorious festival,
  And to express their gratitude, they say,
That all that night in high Valhalla's hall,
  To sound of lutes, they sang a spousal lay;
  And that Iduna, crowned with flowers of May,
With bright-eyed Braga was content to wed;
  And that, the while her apples round her lay,
And poppied pillows propped her fragrant head,
Sweet bridal songs from far, re-echoed round her bed.

BLOWING SOAP-BUBBLES.

An old man stood amid a merry group
  Of children, armed with pipes of clay;
  He had his bloom as well as they;
Musing, he gazed upon their joyous play,
And thus, in frolic rhymes, his buoyant thoughts found way:
    "Keep them dancing high and low;
      Dying dolphins glisten so.
      Make bright rainbows come and go!
      Purse your rosy lips and blow;
      Blow your bubbles, children, blow!"

Sometimes he gazes on an orbéd film,
  Which brightens as it grows more thin;
  More gay than carp with golden fin,
With pictured trees and skies—without—within—
Which mounts—and floats—and bursts upon some dim-
      pled chin.
      Your locks are glossed with morning's glow;
      Whiter are mine than printless snow.
      Your limbs have many a year to grow,
      Mine soon must pay the debt they owe;
      Then blow your bubbles, children, blow."

On each thin globe he views a double picture,
  One *in* the globe and one *upon;*
  One stands erect, inverted one;
A double rack of clouds, a double sun,
Whilst o'er those doubled forms prismatic lusters run.
    "On boundless space your bubbles throw,
      No matter where they're wafted to;
      No seed is lost which true hands sow,
      Full harvest comes, however slow;

The veriest downballs children blow,
    May kill some error, wisdom's foe;
    May kill Conceit and lay him low;
    Then purse your lips, and stand tiptoe—
    Now they are sinking—blow, boys, blow."

And, as when Newton saw the apple fall,
    When Franklin sailed the cloudward kite,
    Vast realms of knowledge gleamed to sight;
Thus did that old man, with supreme delight,
Behold large tracts of truth flash suddenly from night.
    " Deep-channeled thought can ne'er o'erflow;
    Its waves are dashing to and fro;
    It knows no ebb, but only flow;
    Unnumbered truths are yet to know;
    Then blow your bubbles, children, blow."

A BUTTERFLY'S EGG.

A seed! An egg! Who that has mused on these,
    Has not, still musing, held his soul more dear,
    And sworn himself immortal! A small sphere!
A small, round world of untold mysteries!
    An acorn-cup? It holds huge forest trees.
    A bird's egg? Eagle's wings are folded here,
And melodies unheard by mortal ear,
    And plumes unruffled by an earthly breeze.
    What words of wonder in a painted shell!
    And yet, more wonderful to reason's eye
Are those *fine, inconspicuous dots*, which tell
    That in their microscopic globules lie
    Fold within fold encycled, by strange spell,
    Whole orbs of embryo life, types of man's destiny.

FEEDING-TIME IN WINTER IN THE EAST.

A FARMER'S LAY.

Fierce wintry winds but little heeding,
The farmer trudges off to feeding.

From the barn-door in the second story,
He views a scene of purple glory.

All day the clouds looked cold and leaden,
But now along the sky they redden.

Across their colors bright and listed
He sees black trees all gnarled and twisted.

He hears below him cattle lowing,
And marks how well his colts are growing.

Home trots his mare; the smith has shod her.
His farm-boys toss about the fodder.

His grooms rub down the horses' haunches;
The cock and hens creep up the branches.

Ere stars their radiance shall be shedding,
Each beast shall have good food and bedding.

Nor does the farmer leave the stable
Till candles light his supper-table.

Thence to his home so snug and cozy,
To greet his wife and children rosy.

TWO SONNETS.

ADDRESSED TO PROFESSOR J. W. REESE, ON PRESENTING HIM A
STONE CONTAINING CURIOUS IMPRESSIONS.

In order fully to understand the two following sonnets, as well as the objects to which they relate, it may be necessary to inform the reader that the
metallic impressions referred to (by some called "arborisms," by others "den-
drites"), were found *deep inside* the limestone rock (itself originally far under
water-level). The rock itself was first opened by gunpowder, and then sub-
divided by powerful sledge-hammers. The seams or close fissures containing
the pictures were so tight as actually to be in juxtaposition, as if glued together; hence, of each picture there was a duplicate, so wonderful are Nature's
doings in the dark.

I wish I could present you something, Reese,
More worthy your acceptance—something more
Brilliant and rich—some tablet pictured o'er
With mimic ruins, such as never cease
To pique the fancy, and with new increase
Of thought, to add to memory's garnered store—
Some marble marked with shell or madrepore,
Or rare moss-agate flecked with shrubs and trees.
In place of this, lo! pictures on the hard
Coarse limestone, disimprisoned, freed,
Like flowers from winter's thrall upblossoming!
Yet even these are curious. Avon's bard
Would have admired them; for *he* loved to read
" Sermons in stones, and good in everything."
Deep underground, where not the faintest gleam
Of starlight or of sunshine ever stole,
Deeper than haunt of subterranean mole,
Those mystic forms were gendered. Like a dream
They sprang to being. 'Twixt the close-knit seam
Of the thin-fissured limestone, perfect, whole,
Stem, branchlet, twiglet, flow'ret, foliole,

3

In darkness they upstarted. It might seem
As though a subtle fairy of the mine
   Deep-versed in magic arts and elfin lore,
(The whilst she made full many a mystic sign),
   Had melted into drops some choicest ore,
And interposed the rocks with pictures fine
Of ouphant plants and forests crystalline.

THE DRAINING : A FARMER'S LAY.

With loathsome weeds and coarse-stemmed grasses harsh,
On one end of a field a plashy marsh
Too long had pained the careful farmer's eye.
Digging a ditch, he drained the wet land dry,
And soon in place of mud and gelid ooze,
Came tasseled maize, and grain of golden hues,
And fuller barns, and merrier harvest-home.
Soon dripping water flags, and miry foam,
Vanished before the plowshare. Covered drains,
Built strong enough to bear huge six-horse wains,
Gave ample space for salient springs to bound,
Springs which had choked and sobbed beneath the ground
Unknown e'en to the woodcock's probing bill.
And soon each trickling, tributary rill,
Uniting in one channel, fresh and cool,
Came from the earth, a heaven-reflecting pool,
Where dreamy cattle, standing round the brink
In sultry summer days, were seen to drink.
Beholding this, the farmer oft would smile,
And praise the ditcher from the Emerald Isle.

STRANGE SOUNDS HEARD AROUND THE WORLD.

Come, reader, let us wander round the world,
And list sweet Nature's music here and there;
'Twill teach us to believe in Memnon.   First,
Pass we a night by Manitoba Lake
Among the Ojibway Indians.   From the shore
We can descry beneath the moon an islet,
From which, whene'er a gentle north wind blows,
Sweet mystic sounds are wafted o'er the wave,
Rising or sinking as the breezes breathe,
Or die away like distant convent bells
At times, at times like solemn midnight chants
Of nuns at Trinitâ del Monti; wild
And weird the unearthly music floats
Across the waters, like a strain from spirit land.
   The cause is as poetic as the sound:
Along the islet's beach lie hollow shreds
Of limestone, tumbled from the cliff above;
These, beat upon by pebbles small and round
Rolled shoreward by the billows, fill the air
With melody, as though the Master of Life
Were hovering pleased around his favorite haunt,
His moccasins o'erhung with musical shells,
To dance a mystic dance beneath the stars,
And hold creation spellbound.*

*Manitoba Lake, which has given name to the province formed out of the Red River region, is called after a small island, whence, in the stillness of the night, issue strangely sweet, mysterious sounds.   The Ojibway Indians who dwell in that neighborhood believe the island to be the home of Manitoba, the Speaking God, and will not land on or approach it for any consideration, thinking they would desecrate or profane it, and that they would meet with some terrible fate for their impiety.   The sound is caused, it has been ascertained, by the beating of the waves on the large pebbles along the shore.

Now southward turning, wing we our swift flight
O'er Mexico's deep gulf, and o'er the isles
Of India of the West, and posting on
Thought-rapid to the equinoctial line,
We reach the Orelana, mighty stream,
And, wondering, look around us.   Red men there
Point to far Paruguaxo's mountain peaks,
And tell of mystic sounds that there are heard
What time the mountain labors—birth-pangs these,
With clang and flash and uproar through the glens,
Birth-labor, followed, as they fondly hope,
By boundless treasure thrown up from the earth,
Diamonds, and precious stones, and priceless wealth.
Hence, to the genii of those wonder-lands,
And to the thunder spirits of the hills,
They hang rich offerings on the bowing trees,
Or pile them on the cliffs.   In vain, in vain;
Their El Dorado proves an empty dream.*
Next let us visit Madagascar's isle
And listen to the so-called *Devil's Voice*,
Which oft bursts forth in still midsummer nights,
Now from afar, now near, but suddenly,
And startling beyond all power of words
To tell its awful influence on the soul.

These, with fragments of fine-grained, compact limestone that have fallen from
the cliffs above, are rubbed together by the action of the water, and give out a
tone like that of distant church bells. The natural music is heard when the
wind blows from the north, and, as it subsides, low, plaintive notes, resembling
voices of an invisible choir, are heard. It has been compared to the chant of
the nuns at the Trinita del Monti in Rome, with which all travelers are familiar.
The effect is impressive. Tourists have been awakened at night in the vicinity
under the impression that chimes of bells were ringing afar off, and that their
tones were rippling over the lake. The mystic bells of Manitoba have ac-
quired such reputation that travelers are never satisfied unless they are heard,
and often spend days there waiting for the blowing of the north wind. The
Ojibways have a number of poetic legends about their Speaking God, whom
they profoundly revere.—New York Times.

* See Humboldt's Travels in South America.

A creeping terror seizes every heart,
A terror mixed with melancholy—grief
Unutterable masters all the being,
And terrible forebodings.   Seems as though
A planetary spirit, once a man,
Were giving vent to anguish of the damned,
Sometimes in slow, sad measures, sometimes swift
(Then most terrific, when most rapid-sounding),
And petrifying all the heart with awe.*
    Next let us fly, in thought, to Barrey's Isle,†
At the deep Severn's mouth, and pausing there,
Apply the ear to the cliff at a certain point,
And, hist! what noises: bellows blowing loud,
Hammers on anvils ringing all night long,
As though swart gnomes and sooty elves were there,
And long-armed dwarfs expert in handicraft,
And all the clamor of a blacksmith's forge,
Making him mad that listens.

                                    Quick, away!
And winging back our course o'er ocean's wave
And o'er the Mississippi valley, westward still,
Reach we the Rocky Mountains.   There, 'tis said,
At certain places, both by day and night,
Artillery-firing, or what seems to be such,
Rolls booming o'er the plains.   Most strange indeed!
Such, awe-struck, heard the first exploring band
By Lewis and by Clarke led overland;
On Declaration Day they heard the sound,

---

*For some account of this curious phenomenon, see Shubert's Nachtseite der Naturgeschischte.

† At Barrey, an isle of the Severn's mouth, they seem to hear a smith's forge, blowing of bellows and knocking of hammers, if they apply the ear to the cliff.—Burton's Anatomy of Melancholy.

And paused in silent wonder; seemed as though
The eternal mountains strove with one accord
To celebrate our freedom, peal on peal
With deep reverberations echoing far.*

SONNET.

At the dead of night, when universal silence reigned throughout the city, a
silence deepened by the awful thought of the ensuing day, on a sudden was
heard the sound of musical instruments, and a noise which resembled the excla-
mations of Bacchanals. This tumultuous procession seemed to pass through
the whole city, and to go out at the gate which led to the enemy's camp. Such
as reflected upon this prodigy, concluded that Bacchus, the god whom Antony
affected to imitate, had then forsaken him.—Plutarch's Life of Antony, p. 125.

Loud pealed the banquet; rosy Almas sprang
  Across the painted floor on bounding feet;
  Pages ran to and fro; in accents sweet,
To sound of harps, Egyptian minstrels sang;
High up the ceiling laughter echoing rang,
  And naught seemed wanting to their joy complete.
  So crept on midnight.   Then, along the street
Was heard from far the dread and mystic clang
  Of cymbals shrill and shout of Bacchant boys.
Oh! how the guests turned pale, and strove to gaze
  Upon those phantoms, whilst with madd'ning noise
And pipings loud they swept from gate to gate!
  And thus it happens oft; our very *joys*
To unseen Sibyls turn, prophetic of fell fate.

* An account of this curious phenomenon may be seen in the expedition of
Lewis and Clarke, made during the administration of Jefferson. It adds one
more to the number of coincidences relating to the Fourth of July, which, all
taken together, are too striking and numerous ever to be considered the result
of blind chance. Want of time and space prevents me from giving an enumer-
ation of them, but it might repay the reader to search them out for himself.

LITTLE STAR-FLOWER'S SHORT LIFE AND HAPPY DEATH.

ON FINDING A FLOWER OF THE ASTER FAMILY GROWING ON THE TRACK OF A RAILROAD.

Where the railway's track runs deeper
    Through a narrow, rock-bound glen,
Where tall cliffs rise steep and steeper,
Peeped from 'neath a wooden sleeper,
    Star-flower, with her raylets ten.
Not with sheen of gold or scarlet
    Flashing on the wanderer's sight,
    But with *unprismatic* light
Beamed the tiny ten-rayed starlet,
    Masking rainbow hues in *white*.

Sheathing thus the colors seven
    Of God's Peace-bow all in one,
Tranquil days to her seemed given,
Gazing blissful up to heaven
    On God's home—the Central Sun:
And though loads of men and lumber
    O'er her swept on thundering cars,
Wide awake, she seemed to slumber
With her rays of mystic number
    Beaming back, the Star of Stars!

He who, thoughtful, might observe her
    Ere her blossom 'gan to ope,
    Ere she gazed on heaven's cope,
Would have seen *one* color serve her,
    One—the hue of youthful Hope.

Green her flower-cup, green: five-parted ?
  Five ? a type for her unmeet;
  Green ? her being's springtide sweet, ,
Till, in few more hours, outstarted
  Full-orbed whiteness, pure, complete.

Worlds above her, Earth below her,
  Drinking sunlight, quaffing dew,
Death came sudden to o'erthrow her: *
View her, Poet, you may know her;
  Dead, she yet may speak to you;
Telling, how beneath the rushing
  Wheels of labor, oft are found
Human flow'rets, sweetly blushing,
Star-allied, and kept from crushing
  By their nearness to the ground.

BURNING BRUSH: A FARMER'S LAY.

Year after year yon barren hill,
Haunt of the plaintive whip-poor-will,
Unfit for pasture and for plow,
Has reared aloft its sterile brow,
Each springtide with wild violets blooming,
Each rosy summer eve vocal with Night-hawk's booming.
    But, lo! to-night,
    Most cheering sight!
My children from my porch in wonder gazing,
    See light on light,
    Each one more bright,
Along the barren hilltop upward blazing.

* Be it known to all who take an interest in such weighty matters, that the death of the sweet floweret was occasioned by the writer's plucking it up by the roots, to send by mail to Mr. Longfellow in company with the above poem.

Along the sedge and sallow grass,
  Now looming large, now almost hid
  Behind some quivering pyramid,
I see tall forms pass and repass,
Tossing on heaps of sassafras
        Old gnarled roots and thorny briars,
        To feed the fires,
        And build the pyres,
The funeral pyres of yellow Barrenness;
And as each lofty pile outflashes
  It leaves behind most fertilizing ashes.

All this the farmer views with pleased emotion.
      But mark! how ever higher—higher—
        All alone
        One fiery cone
Shoots spirally aloft with corkscrew motion,
        Madly whirling,
        Fiercely twirling
        Amidst frantic
Blasts and currents round it eddying,
            Ever more and more gigantic,
    Till, having reached its stature full,
Its own red column firmly steadying,
      It stands for a moment immovable.
Oh, how its bowing brothers court it!
      And as some mighty Mind,
      Rising above its kind,
      Itself creates the circling gust
      Which lifts it towering from the dust,
      So does that fiery shaft,   -
      As if with sense of power it madly laughed,
Itself create the stormy currents that support it.

THE INVALID'S MORNING WATCH IN WINTER.

Lo! shadowy forms gigantic,
  As the flames ascend or fall,
Dance many a long-legged antic
  O'er ceiling and o'er wall.

Far distant ghosts seem sailing,
  Faint death-bells strike the ear;
'Tis but the damp logs wailing
  On erring fancy's ear.

Like coals half quenched in ashes
  The panes loom leaden-gray,
And slow the penciled sashes
  Their checker-work display.

On narrower inspection,
  A tree's faint-shadowed trunk
Looms through the window's section,
  Almost to dimness sunk.

Thus slowly, slowly rocking
  In my old ancestral chair,
Thought after thought comes flocking
  Till twilight paints the air.

And when young Dawn comes launching
  Her crimson boats of cloud,
Yon tree, before unbranching,
  And draped in sable shroud,

Towers high in glory, sainted
  By halos bright of rays;
Trunk, bough, and twig all painted
  On a ground of golden haze.

So, when the sky above us
  Gleams bright'ning in its track,
The angels seem to love us
  And drive ill demons back.

THE LOVER'S WHISPERING GALLERY UNDER THE SEA.

I've heard of galleries, galleries submarine,
Which lovers secretly, sweetly may whisper in,
Where winged syllables fleetly are wafted through,
Swift as the lightning's flash cleaves a black cloud in two.
Come, my beloved one! speak to me, speak to me!
How my heart throbs to thee through the vast hungry sea!

Where huge leviathans sport, far, far from either shore,
We may hold converse sweet over old Ocean's floor;
Over drowned argosies, o'er sunken treasure ships;
Speak to me, speak to me, with thy fresh rosy lips!

Deep under mountain waves, deep under tossing brines,
Far 'neath the touch of the sailor's deep sounding line,
Far as salt billows boom, far as tides ebb and flow,
Loving thoughts wander now, aye, flashing to and fro.
Then, though between us, love, storm-beaten ocean roll,
Speak to me—stream to me—flash through my inmost soul!

SONNET.

OF MEN AND PLANETS, EACH SEEMS SUBJECT TO A TWOFOLD REVOLUTION.

As earth sustains a twofold motion—one
　　Urging it ever round its own fixed pole,
　　The other causing it for aye to roll
Around the central, all-supporting sun,
Whence day and night in due succession run
Their rounds, with change of seasons; thus the soul
Of man, by laws beyond her own control
　　Is by a twofold impulse driven on.
A self-encircling, God-attracted sphere
　　She is, with one side dark and one side bright,
Sin's shadow there, celestial radiance here,
　　Here summer morn, there starless, wintry night.
But, O! what joy, when near and still more near
　　Attracted, she shall be absorbed in God's own light.

THE MYSTIC MIRROR.

In a chamber hushed and dark
　　Hangs a mirror now for show;
Lovely lady, come and gaze!
Long before the solar rays
Glisten round the soaring lark,
　　O'er its surface, to and fro
　　Thronging figures come and go;
Self-illumed they appear,
Some afar, and some anear,
　　Some in never-ending row
Reaching backward to the sea.
Come, fair lady, gaze with me!

On its surface hyaline
  I can see a vision now
  Clearly pictured—so canst thou.
I see mourners round a grave
O'er which weeping willows wave;
And a coffin black as night
  Sinking lower, lower down;
Now it disappears from sight
  Mournfully, beneath the moon.
Weep, fair lady, for full soon
Clods shall tumble on the lid,
  And young eyes, erst starry bright,
  Shall be covered from the light;
And those beauties shall be hid,
  Which we all did idolize.
  Lay her low; for she shall rise
  At the Resurrection Day.
Dead-asleep the *body* lies;
Lark-like, the *soul* ascends the skies:
  Weep no more, lady fair, I pray;
  Come away, come away.

SOMETHING ALMOST TOO SILLY FOR VERSE.

One sunny morn, in early May,
I wandered far in the woods astray,
And beheld two beautiful birds at play.

Like glittering shuttles of golden hue
They shot the blossomed branches through,
And fluttering, disappeared from view.

When next I passed, my eyes were blessed
With the sight of a wingéd one on her warm nest.
But how many eggs she had—she knew best.

THE TWO SISTERS.

Although the Morning and the Evening Star,
   When first they strike upon the gazer's sight,
   Seem equal in intensity and light,
Yet do they call forth thoughts dissimilar.
The one, soft-throbbing in the west afar,
   Suits best the mood of pensive Eremite;
   The other, is the hunter's dear delight;
Thus, to my eyes, those lovely Sisters are.
One, like a pious nun, whose beads are told,
   Seems wrapt in high communion with the skies,
   With folded palms, and upward-gazing glance;
The other, has sheen glossy curls of gold,
   Sweet laughing lips, and still more laughing eyes,
   And dimples gay, and feet that love the dance.

EASTER EGGS.

As yet no swallows give each other chase,
   No oriole yet her airy hammock weaves,
The flower with blood-red juice and pallid face*
     Still sleeps beneath dead leaves.
But silvery clouds, afloat in freshest blue,
   Cast flying shadows o'er the greening hills,
The scarlet maple flowering bursts to view,
     And yellow daffodils.
New flowers, new birds, new heavens, a fresh new earth!
   Celestial raptures and the joy of joys!

           * The Sanguinaria.

God's Easter comes to glad with holy mirth
  Old men and laughing boys.
Bright eggs! Behold them by each path, each street,
  The gay, the million-pictured, rainbow-hued!
O'er all the land young fingers, rosy-sweet,
  Uplift the heavenly food.
Come and partake! Within those painted shells
  Is found the core of many precious things—
Bird-music sweeter than the sweetest bells,
  And embryo angel-wings.
Partake in faith! And from the sacred feast
  Shall rise within thee a new morning star,
More bright than that which guided in the East
  The wise men from afar.

TO A NIGHT-HAWK.

Whilst amidst branches fresh and leaves high hung
  The oriole swings her hammock, thou art found,
  Hoarse Night-Hawk, on the bare and barren ground,
Lank-waving sedge and sallow weeds among,
All day lone-brooding. But when Eve has flung
  Her twilight mantle o'er her, all around
  Yon grave-yard hill with shrill and booming sound
Madly thou wheelest, whilst thy shapeless young
Lie on the earth unsheltered. Bird of gloom!
  Dark specter of the woods! I fain would know
Whether no gleams of pleasure e'er illume
  Thy shadowy life, or when thy trump of woe
Moans on the hill, or when on woodland tomb
  Folding thy white-barred wings, thou crouchest low.

THE FLIGHT INTO EGYPT.

Σῷ δὲ θρόνῳ πυρόεντι παρεστᾶσιν πολυμόχθοι
᾽Αγγελοι οἷσι μέμηλε βροτοῖς ὡς πάντα τέλειται.

Orphic Hymn.

Around God's fiery throne, with sleepless ken,
Angelic watchers guard the ways of men.

4

THE FLIGHT INTO EGYPT.

BOOK I.

HOLYLAND.

CANTO I.

THE FLIGHT COMMENCES—OLD BATTLE-FIELD SEEN BY A NEW LIGHT.

A WAKING VISION of the Flight to Egypt!
To view heaven's orbs by daylight, men were wont,
In olden times, to visit some deep well,
Or the dusk crypt of some vast pyramid,
Whence, looking up, they could, through one small open-
    ing,
Behold the stars at noon, and e'en descry
The pole-star's culmination.   Thus may we,
Dim-sighted from the glare of common day,
Enter the shadowy Cave of Waking Dreams,
And kneeling reverent on the marble floor,
Behold, through one small opening—O, the joy!
The Star of stars, the star that leads to Christ.

A Waking Vision of the Flight to Egypt!
Come, listen: though the words be poor and weak,
Weak and imperfect, like all earthly things,
The VISION, if heaven-born, may glimmer through them,
As sinking sunlight gleams through some old oak.
  Full eighteen months had passed since Christ was born,
Most of which time was spent at Nazareth,
The home of Mary and the foster-sire.
Then Joseph and the Mother of the Child,
As was their frequent custom, paid a visit
To their relations in the hill-country.
Whilst there, the Angel of the Lord appeared
To Joseph in a dream, and said: "Arise,
Take the young Child in haste, and take the mother,
And, fleeing into Egypt, be thou there
Until I bring thee word; for Herod seeks
To take the young Child's life."
                            Joseph arose,
Obedient to the messenger's command,
And journeyed on towards Egypt.
                            Night was coming;
The new moon, thin and small, could scarce be seen;
It seemed a silver sickle, edgewise viewed,
Soft melting in the sunset's golden glow
Like pearl melting in wine. All night the stars,
God's brightest thoughts addressed to human eyes,
Rose in the east and sank below the west,
In clustered constellations wonderful.
The Northern Cross sloped o'er Judea's hills,
Job's Coffin hung as if self-poised o'erhead,
The Sickle glittered with its starry curve,
And lovelier still, fair clustering down the west,
The silvery Sisters Seven, o'er Rachel's tomb
Seemed mourning for their lost one.

Paths obscure
And unfrequented ways they first pursued,
Lest Herod's all but bloodhounds, all unleashed
And rabid for the scent of human blood,
Might follow on their footsteps.   A long journey,
A drear and perilous journey, lay before them,
Danger in front and dangers in the rear,
And many a weary waste of desert land.

Well Joseph knew each road and every farm
For many a mile round Ephratah; as boy
He had explored them oft in company
Of some dear kinsfolk of the hill country,
Whilst visiting his blood-relations there.

So on they journeyed, hushed, but fast at first,
Afraid to whisper much above their breath,
Threading small, tortuous sheep-tracks wild and rough,
By many a silent vineyard, many a grove,
Past olive gardens, grain fields, ancient oaks,
Past mountains caverned into antique tombs,
Past slumbering villages, whose inmates lay
Couched on the housetops oriental-wise,
Soft dreaming, sweet asleep beneath the stars.

At last they reached a mount whose lofty brow
Was overshadowed by a branching grove
Of terebinth; which having passed, behold
Before them in the dark what seemed a vale
With streamlet in the midst, and hills beyond.

"Behold the vale of Elah," Joseph said,
And pointed with his staff.   The Virgin looked,
But all seemed dim and shadowy to her eye,
Veiled o'er by shrouding night.
Sudden, an instantaneous pulse of light,
Unlike all other light from fire or sun,
From glowworm, planet, or enchanted lamp,

Streamed wave on wave in undulations strange,
O'erflowing the horizon's utmost rim.
    It was indeed that memorable vale
Where, more than ten long centuries before,
A shepherd lad, with staff and sling and bag,
A rosy boy, fresh from his father's flocks,
Had gathered five smooth pebbles from the brook,
Wherewith to slay the giant.
The Virgin gazed entranced.   Her full, large eyes,
Swimming in liquid rapture, rolled around,   .
Taking in either mountain at a glance,
And all the windings of the brook, which now,
For lack of rain, was shrunk within its channel
With wave-worn stones and pebbles overheaped.
Those pebbles had been swept by many a flood
Down from the neighboring mountains on each side,
And where the stream was fullest, disappeared.
    But that strange light!   Scarce could the Virgin tell
Which most to wonder at, the mystic light
Itself, or the weird scene it shone upon,
Bringing out every object into view,
And giving all a beauty not its own.
To her it seemed as though the glorious bow
Around God's throne, the rainbow of high heaven,
Were melted into radiance pearly white,
And having fused its *seven* hues into *one*,
That one were streaming on a snow-white dove,
Whose every wing-flap sent a wave of brightness
In undulating currents round the globe.
Nor was that all.   She heard, or thought she heard
At intervals, a fine unearthly chime
Caught only by the spirit's inner ear,
Which marvelously seemed to sink or swell
With the light's ebb and flow, and to embrace,

In full harmonic unity, each tone,
Each melody conceivable by man,
Into a sevenfold twine of woven sound,
Which sometimes sevenfold seemed, and sometimes three
    As when in early spring a throng of clouds
Sweep hurrying overhead, some silver-edged,
Some streaked by penciled beams, which radiate,
Spoke-like, all streaming from a central point
(That point close-clouded, center of the wheel),
Some shaped like floating turrets set adrift,
And all, in endless sequence casting down
A host of racing shadows o'er green hills;
Such, and so masque-like, was the throng of thoughts
Which drifted o'er the Virgin's fresh young soul.
    Joseph, who had been kneeling, rose and cried
In solemn utterance, quoting from the Book:
"God said, let there be light, and light there was."
Then long and deep he gazed upon *her* eyes,
As though all heaven were mirrored in their orbs,
Heaven behind heaven, in far perspective view;
He gazed on her; *she* on the Primal Light.
Then on they passed o'er that old battle-field
Until they reached the brook.   There Joseph stooped,
And from the smooth white stones reposing there
Gathered an egg-shaped pebble, water-worn,
And, save for its suggestions, little worth.
"Doubtless 'twas much like this," he, musing, said,
Holding the smooth stone in his outstretched palm,
And lapsing into meditative smile,
Half quaint, half reverent, "much like this, I ween,
And picked up, mayhap, from the self-same spot.
A thing like this?   A plaything of the flood?
A bauble for a boy to sling at birds?
No wonder that Goliah laughed to scorn

At first the slinger and the thing he slung.
Yet, in my inmost heart I do believe—"
And as he spoke an earnestness profound
Deepened his tones, and flushed his manly cheek,
"That He "—he pointed to the Heavenly Babe,
And bowed, and reverently clasped his hands—
"That He, the manger-cradled, cattle round Him,
Will, in due time, confront and do to death
An Anakim ten million times more dread
Than him whom David slaughtered with a sling:
Nay, with a thing of simple, common use.
A simple word or two, The Word—no more—
Shall work such wonders through all coming times,
That future generations without end,
In ever new developments, shall grow
And grow into more rich and perfect bloom,
Until Humanity's full-blossoming flower,
Never full blown, but always blossoming,
Shall be transplanted into heaven's high fields,
And mix its odors with the flowers above."

    So saying, he tossed the pebble back.   They three
Traversed the channel of the shrunken stream,
And as they journeyed on, might be compared
To holy thoughts in penitent human souls
Calm moving on where storms have left their mark.
A Holy Family journeying through the night!
Two human; *One* both human and divine;
The foster-father faithful, good and true,
The Virgin Mother all-immaculate,
The incarnate God in budding infancy,
All Three mysteriously linked in love,
Love such as angels scarce can comprehend!

    The humblest things of earth oft shadow forth
In some sweet way the ineffable things of heaven,

And lowly plants trod down by cloven hoofs
And browsed by cattle, show to pious eyes
The mystic symbols of a higher life.
Then pardon me, I pray, if I compare
That Holy Family, that trinal group,
To something noticed in our daily walks.
Wander some summer morn adown the meads
Or o'er the pastured hills, before the dew
Has by the sun been quaffed; you chance may spy
A three-leaved clover, with a delicate ring
Or mystic circle curving o'er the leaves,
So curving as to form a perfect round.
'Twould seem almost as though Divinity,
To write its gospel underneath our feet,
Had chosen this small plant, and had impressed
Upon the embryo petals, ere their birth,
This symbol form, most perfect of all forms,
A miniature impress of God's signet-ring.
Each leaf, though separate, bears its segment due,
And all combined compose the rounded whole.
So far each seems to bear an equal share
Of the divine. But of the three, should *one*
Have on it a small drop of common dew,
A common dewdrop, loveliest thing on earth,
A tiny globule like an opal-stone,
Or like one of those strange oracular gems
Which shone of old upon the high priest's breastplate,
Self-luminous, outsparkling, all aglow
With the Shekinah glory—that *one leaf,*
Though fed by juice from the same earthly root,
And bearing on its face the self-same mark,
Outshines them all. No more: you understand.
Then as the three went calmly journeying on,

The Virgin thus, in meditative mood,
Expressed her thoughts aloud.
                              "O, what a night!
I thank thee, my Creator, for this night.
The very danger adds a zest to joy.
Those stars above us seem not common stars;
This earth we tread on seems like a new earth;
That tuft of palm-trees, waving from afar,
Fans the bland air like trees of Paradise;
And more than all, this strange, delicious light,
So softly penetrant, so crystal clear,
So fringed with faintly-tinted stellar rainbows,
Streams through my soul, and seems to wash away
All spots and stains flesh had engendered there.
    See how the infant Savior scans the stars,
How his large, innocent eyes are fixed aloft!
Perhaps this wondrous light may come from him.
But once before, once only did I see
Such light; it was the night that He was born.
And hark! these strains from yonder distant hill,
Where shepherds watch their flocks!—the same, the same—
The song the angels taught them on that night.
I thank thee, my Creator, for that song—
Glory to God! O, glory in the highest!
On earth be peace, and good-will toward men."
    Some moments paused the travelers, to hear
That pastoral anthem floating round the hills,
That echo of a song composed in heaven,
And when again the chorus pealed from far,
With one accord, then, Joseph and the Virgin,
One sinking to a deep and manly bass,
The other mounting lark-like, silver-toned,
Hand clasped in hand and voice with voice commingled,
They joined the shepherds in that song of praise,

The whilst high heaven's golden portals opened,
And such a stream of harmony august,
Commixed with voices high-angelical,
Pealed downwards through the peopled orbs of space,
In unison with music of the spheres,
That the whole universe through all its breadth
And height and depth grew tremulous with joy,
And as the diapason rolled along,
Those heaven-sweet words could still be heard through all,
Glory to God, O, glory in the highest!
On earth be peace, and good-will toward men!

CANTO II.

AMONG THE SHEPHERDS.

DESCEND we now from these empyreal heights,
Where human spirits dare not linger long,
And liken what has faintly been described
To things, though earthlier, easier to conceive.
As in that fairy city of the sea,
For its Rialto famed and Bridge of Sighs,
Whose streets are waves, whose wains are gondolas,
Two centuries ago, on moonlight nights,
Two gondoliers, at fitting space apart,
Sung in alternate strophes, loud and clear,
But sweetly pensive, Tasso's epic song,
Chanting of battles fought in Holy Land,
And how Jerusalem was won, how won
The tomb of Christ, with how much toil and blood—
If, then, in midst of their responsive notes,
All of a sudden, some sweet chime of bells,
Or sacred carillon from neighboring church

Or campanile, church quick answering church,
Rung far and wide, the charm was all complete,
Still stood the wanderer on the airy bridge,
Thronged were all balconies, and every barge,
Each pinnace floating o'er the rapt lagoon,
Seemed spellbound by the music.

*   *   *   *   *   *   *

Gradual that spheral melody died away,
Starting afresh whene'er some planet rose,
Or rounding up into an arch of sound
At every culmination of a star
Of more than usual mark—then dying down
To silence at the setting of some world
Which sank with all its anthems down the west
In ever-lessening cadence. Petty thoughts,
By earth engendered and to earth confined,
Were overflooded by an astral tide
Of meditations broad as utmost stretch
Of galaxies and zodiacs curved beyond
The scope of mortal vision. Gradual, too,
The superhuman light became more dim,
Leaving an amber twilight on the earth
More pearly than the radiance of the moon,
But fainter, too, and ever growing fainter,
The whilst the travelers slowly journeyed on.

   At last they reached a point where many roads
Like branches from a larger trunk shoot off,
To various points diverging.   Joseph paused
And fixed his eyes upon the stars, intently
Gazing, as helmsman in mid-ocean scans
His compass, thus instructed how to steer
To some far distant port.   Then, as he gazed,
His head, till now so clear, became confused;
He wist not where to turn, when, all at once,

The Infant Savior raised his little hand,
Smiled with a roseate smile, and pointed up.
Behold! extending on above the line
Of one of those five roads, appeared a band
Of wingéd seraphs sporting in mid-air,
Now seen and now unseen, in varying show.
Their airy plaything seemed a curious ball,
Striped with seven listed hues, like heaven's own bow,
Which, when in motion, tossed from hand to hand,
And swiftly circling, made one curving stream
Of whitest light, most lovely to behold;
But which, when held quiescent in the grasp,
Gleamed with a sevenfold radiance. O, how fair
Those seraph faces glowed, face behind face!
How beautiful beyond conception's reach,
Yon rounding circle, in the act of forming,
At first seems shifting quick in rapid whirl,
And then, with wings outstretched, tip touching tip,
Stands fixed a moment—soon to be dissolved.
Anon, a pair of seraphs rise aloft
In spiral curves, the whilst another pair,
With wings alike in coloring and in size,
Seem wafted downwards. Spectacle jocose,
Which pleased the Infant's eye and made him laugh.
As when at noontide, o'er some quiet lake,
We mark a brace of painted butterflies
Wheeling around each other up the air,
The whilst a second painted pair is seen
Below the wave, now wafted up, now down,
Inversely as the first pair sinks or mounts.
  Scarce seven short seconds did the vision last,
And during that delicious span of time,
It three times seven appeared and disappeared,
The loveliest coming last; for e'er it fled,

A plumed half-circle of seraphic forms,
In number Thirty-one, with wings half-closed,
All bowing with their heads, on bended knees
In graceful poise, looked down, and kissed their hands.
The Virgin kissed hers, too, and kissed the Child's,
Whilst Joseph stroked his beard and grateful smiled.
She then, with cheek upon the Savior's cheek,
Soft touching soft, and fair with fair conjoined,
Thus cheerily spoke in accents mirthful sweet:
"How oft—it seems indeed but yesterday—
Whilst yet a little child, in early spring,
Have I, on some sweet morning, danced and sung
On the tall hilltop near to Nazareth,
Now gazing towards Carmel and the sea,
Now glancing over Esdraelon's plain
To Lebanon capped with snow.   How often, then,
In frolic circles whirling round and round,
Have we—I mean the girls of Nazareth—
Quite giddy with glad motion, fallen plumb down
Along the daisied turf, panting and laughing,
And all intoxicate with innocent joy,
Whilst the swift wheeling landscape seemed to spin—
The sea, the plain, far Carmel's nodding top,
And Lebanon's white-crowned summits.   O, the joy!
I never thought such scenes would come again,
Such innocence in union with such sport.
Those wingéd ball-players! how they snatched my soul
Above the earth, and wafted me into
The mood of early girlhood.   O, the joy!"
   Joseph, refreshed both by the skyey vision
And by the Virgin's vision-painting words,
Moved onwards south by east with step secure.
"With such a merry pilotage," he said,
"I could contented tread around the earth,

Nor ever feel fatigue." Then with a laugh,
The whilst he glanced at the white donkey near him,
"E'en lumpish Labor pricks up his long ears
And moves with brisker pace, when frolic Mirth
And Merriment lead the way."
    For two hours then they journeyed without halt,
Ever ascending ridge on airy ridge,
Till through a cloven opening in the crags
The road wound downwards. Huge top-heavy cliffs
On one side rose sky-high above their heads,
And on the other yawned a dread abysm,
Through which a mountain torrent chafed and moaned
As if half mad, half doleful. *"Pass of Death,"*
The peasants round had called it in their fear.
Chill night-winds sang their requiem through its pines,
Owls hooted, serpents hissed, and jackals howled,
Whilst, from the highest precipice aloft
Down to the lowest bowlder earthquake-wrenched,
A darkling horror brooded night and day,
And harrowed every soul that entered there.
A narrow mule-path wormed the dizzy side,
Where one false step were death. With shuddering fear
The wanderers entered in that dolorous gorge,
But when the mystic light which shone before
Illumined them again, their hearts were cheered,
And both burst forth into that glorious psalm,
"The Lord my shepherd is—I shall not want,"
Which he and Mary, in alternate chants,
Sang, passing through "The Valley of Death's Shade."
    Another hour of travel brought them to
A little band of shepherds on a hill,
Who chanced to be the same who, on the night
When Christ was born, were first to hail their Lord.
From hilltop on to hilltop they had roamed

In search of pasture, ever moving south,
Until, with all their flocks, their kith and kin,
They reached that far-famed ancient border-land
Near Hebron, which the Patriarchs dearly loved.
At once they recognized their Savior Lord,
And gathering round, with shepherd's staff in hand,
They worshiped Him again on reverent knees.
Among them was a father, son, and son's son;
One, with long locks besprinkled thick with gray;
Another, with black hair and raven beard;
The third, with hazel ringlets clustering round
His roseate cheeks, his chin as smooth as girl's.
So David must have looked when yet a lad;
And to complete the likeness, the boy bore
A sling and staff, and on the harp could play.
Zadoc his name; beloved wherever known.
O, how his eyes were riveted on the Child!
How oft he clasped his hands and bent his knees,
How tears chased smiles across his lovely face!

Now, when they heard the cause of Joseph's flight,
They marveled much. At last the father said:
"Here you may rest secure. Zadoc, conduct
The travelers to the chambers in the rock."

Zadoc obeyed, and at a watch-fire near,
Lighting a pine torch, led them down a path
Which wound 'mong lonely hills, and reaching soon
A cavern's mouth, from which outran a stream
Of purest water, guided them along
From chamber on to chamber, up and down,
By sparry column and 'neath fretted roof
(Stalactite and stalagmite touching hands),
Until he reached the last and largest room
Of all those broad apartments—circular
Its form, with high-arched dome for ceiling. There,

Couched on a mossy bed, that smelt of flowers
And aromatic mountain herbs, there lay
An old, old man, father of that old man
Who watched the sheep outside. An opening through
The center of the dome let starlight in
And smoke of torchlight out. Asleep, 'mid flowers,
There lay the hoary Patriarch, with smooth crown,
And silvery beard and side-locks; wreath of snow
He seemed, fresh fallen on flowers; wreath doomed to
  melt
And vanish soon from earth. With second sight
He now was gifted; twice had cut his teeth;
Thus furnished with the means, before he left
This lower world, to see and taste its charms;
Short foretaste of a lovelier world above.
Perhaps aroused by touch of some sweet dream,
Perhaps by Zadoc's torch, perhaps transpierced
By that soft penetrant and primal light
Which shone before the moon or any star,
The old man started to his feet, and stood
Bolt upright, gazing raptured on the Child,
With arms stretched forth and long beard streaming down,
His eyes aglow with second-sighted fire,
And cried aloud: "Hail! Day-spring from on high."
Then on his knees he fell and clasped his hands,
Zadoc beside him kneeling with his torch,
And Joseph looking on with wondering smile,
Whilst the calm Virgin, folding to her heart
The Infant Jesus, heavenward gazed and prayed.
Then Joseph took the torch from Zadoc's hand
With gentlest touch, and, stepping to one side,
Dipped it within a cistern standing near;
Whereat the effluence of that Other Light
Outstreamed with unstained splendor, filling all

5

The caverned rooms, the limpid spring, the dome,
The old man's shining crown and silvery beard,
And raying upwards through a hole in the dome,
Like an inverted cone, whose base was heaven,
Added to all the stars within its cirque
A super-stellar luster.   "Wonderful!
Can this be heaven indeed?   How beautiful!"
Said the old shepherd, sinking on his couch
Exhausted by the shock of ecstasy,
And lapsing into sweet Elysian dreams,
From which he never woke in this lone world.
But Zadoc knew not the old man was dead,
And still with pious tendance, from a basket
Heaped fresh and fresher sweets upon the limbs
Of his progenitor, and said: "Good night,
Happy good night, and happy be thy waking!"
With other mountain herbs and flowers he spread
A couch on the other side of the caverned fount,
Where, in soft, fragrant coolness, with the Child
The Virgin slept; whilst Joseph, at her feet,
Wearied with toilsome tramping through the night,
Sank from a heaven of dreams to slumber blank,
Like skylark sinking from morn's gorgeous clouds
Down to the clodded earth.   Here let us pause.

CANTO III.

A BLESSING FROM INFANT LIPS.

EARLY they started on their next day's tour.
Joseph had loved the morning all his life;
He loved it now at forty.   Silvery skeins,
Infrequent yet, like threads of thinnest frost

Or fringing snow on glossy evergreens,
Commenced to seam his locks, still black and full.
Like berries seemed they in first autumn-tide.
His forty years had faded not his bloom,
Had spared the blush-rose carmine of his cheeks;
The fresher they for those slight skeins of snow.
Symmetrical his limbs and large of mold,
With nose shaped aquiline, but not too much,
With eyes both dark and bright, dream-beaming, large
(All wide awake and open-orbed, though dreamy),
With mouth which likewise opened easily,
Keeping good time and measure with his eyes;
(When they laughed, that laughed too—a laugh sincere).
One would have taken him for a guileless man,
Core-sound in soul and body—through and through,
A man whom all men trusted—true as steel.
His broad, high forehead seemed the dome of thought,
And rose above his sanguine-tinted cheeks
As some pure marble temple, round at top,
Rises at eventide above a stream
On which the blood-red clouds have cast their glow.
High self-command, that crown of all that's good,
Strong in his youth, and strengthening year by year,
Moon-like and cold itself, and chastely pure;
But, like the moon, brimful of subtlest power,
Now governed all the ebbs and flows of his blood,
As Cynthia governs ocean; so that both
His blood and th' ocean wave, by God-formed laws,
With no stagnation cursed, or torpid calm,
Pulsing in finely modulated rhythm,
In ebb or flow, aye kept their healthful dance.
His trade, too—wonder not at that, my friend,
His trade had passed with healthful influence
Into his brain and heart, and helped to feed

Them both to greater purity and strength.
The carpenter, like the mason, makes his tools
(Or he may make them if he will) his types,
His emblems, and the load-stars of his life.
The compasses, and that which they describe,
The plumb-line, the chalked cord, the rule, the saw,
The gimlet, auger, broadax, hatchet, plane,
All these, could they but speak, would tell a tale
Enforcing or imparting some great truth,
Which, moving from the workman's hand to his heart,
Like sap from root to tree-top, would inform
And fill the whole with vigor, life and light.
Nor is this all; the brain is often tasked;
The man must form exemplars in his mind
Unseen, before the outward work appears;
Must calculate, must measure, must forecast,
Must strive to fathom numbers' wond'rous laws,
The laws which govern geometric forms,
And mastering them, unconsciously imbibes
The deep and holy symbolism they contain.
And so it was with Joseph; his good trade,
Firm following nature's plan, had fashioned him
In symmetry complete, inside and out,
To manhood's finest type.
                                 He had worked in his youth
With many hundred skillful carpenters,
His friends and compeers some, some foreigners,
On the new temple which King Herod built
To God on Mount Moriah.   Few could there
Excel him in design or execution,
And none with quicker insight could embrace
The general plan or master the details;
So that henceforward, to the end of life,
The whole fair structure, with its outer walls,

Its various gates, with all their names, its courts,
Court above court, with numbered steps to mount,
Its altars for burnt-offering or for incense,
Its brazen sea, its lavers, and its fonts,
The Holy Place, with all that there belonged,
And all the various Temple furniture,
Hung like a living picture in his mind,
Warm, life-like, vivid.
Often, with eyes firm closed or in the dark,
These images, with all their hidden meanings,
Rose to his soul, like visions from the sea
Beheld by prophet or inspired seer,
Until his spirit, like a hallowed fane,
Became aglow with consecrated thoughts,
And his words streamed like incense.
                              Such had been
His wont, while still a workman in the temple,
And when his thoughts and fancies all were shaped
By what he wrought on.   Higher views since then
Had dawned upon his soul, a holier Star
Had risen.   Visions heavenly sweet he had
Of a Celestial Temple, not of wood
Or stone, nor built by human hands, of which
The first was but a shadow, soon to pass.
Hence, all the later branchings of his soul
Were brighter than the first, and nearer heaven.
   Conceptions drawn from objects of the earth
Oft aid the mind in grasping thoughts divine;
Swings are they, hung on boughs of earthly trees,
To waft us nearer to the trees of heaven.
One more similitude may make all plain,
Reflecting, like a mirror, Joseph's soul.
Behold yon antique sycamore, which stands
On yonder rounded knoll, above a stream

Where once a furnace stood, in days gone by;
We can behold it from this pillared porch;
('Tis not like sycamores of Palestine,
But such as grow in this, our Western World.)
Bronze seems its trunk, and bronzed the *lower* limbs
All downward twisted, pointing to the earth,
And casting twisted shadows on the bole
In the clear light of morn; the *upper* boughs—
See how they glisten heavenward, amber-white,
Like purest alabaster, tapering fine,
From all sides beckoning *upwards !*
A grand old tree to look on at all times!
But most of all, on some calm autumn eve,
When, having shed its leaves, its form stands out
More prominent against the western heavens.
See, how the sky-line of yon distant hills
Cuts its huge bulk in twain! How black *below*
The severing line shows the swart shadowy trunk,
Whilst all *above*, in clearest tracery drawn,
The ivory boughs, with all their pendent balls
And intricate branch-work, hang in rosy air
As if self-poised. Such, viewed in its totality, appears
To the mind's eye, the tree of Joseph's life,
Seen from our present standpoint. Lo! again
The vision mounts before me, and I follow.

Early they started on their morning journey.
The Patriarch, they supposed, was sweet asleep,
And Zadoc lay, all prostrate, on his face,
As though, whilst kneeling, he had lost his poise,
And thus had sunk to slumber. "Better thus,
Than roused before his time," said Joseph, softly,
And led the Virgin from the silent cave.

Outside, all things were rousing into life,
Cocks crowing, cattle lowing, caroling birds

Astir on every tree-top—freshening airs
Shook every leaf, and, whispering with soft breath,
Called on the sun to rise above the hills.
The ass they found still tethered on the mead,
Where he had browsed some hours on dewy grass,
Now fresh for morning travel.
                              Joseph had,
Before they left the town of Ephratah,
Fashioned a saddle with much care and skill,
Cushioned and draped and nicely stuffed and lined,
So as but little to oppress the beast,
And give the rider a soft, easy seat.
Chairlike its form, and there sat the Madonna,
As painters represent Cassiopeia,
High-seated on her chair near Cepheus old,
Her feet on th' Arctic Circle.   There she sat
In graceful attitude, and glanced around
On all the varying landscapes which they passed,
Without or jolt or jar to vex her thought,
Or interrupt her meditative mood;
By day, her face close veiled, with openings twain
Through which her eyes beamed starlike, whilst at night
The veil was drawn, so that the holy stars
Might gaze on something holier than themselves.
   In this guise moved they on.   Ere long they passed
A cottage, where, beneath a trellised bower,
Wreathed and o'erhung with clustering vines, they saw
Two women at a hand-mill grinding corn;
One threw the grains by gradual handfuls in,
The other turned the mill with pleasing toil;
Each in alternate strophes sang one song,
While both joined in the chorus as it came.
As this went on, the master of the house
And his fair spouse were kneeling on the roof,

With faces turned toward the Holy Place,
Absorbed in morning prayer; thus was prepared
Their daily bread, not without orisons
And many a matin chant, sweet to the ear.
  " Lovely," said Joseph, musing, " even yet,
Is this fair spot, once called the Promised Land; ﹀
How much more lovely once. But Palestine,
Before with downward lapse she reach decay,
Will, if the prophets tell us truly, shed
An effluence from her like the sinking sun,
Which, as he sinks, illumines other lands."
  " Yea," answered Mary, smiling with her eyes,
(Her words rang silver-sweet behind the veil,)
" As westering sun, when storms are past or passing,
Calls forth a lovely rainbow opposite,
So, of this Promised Land, the sinking sun
Will, as his orb declines, transfer the Promise
From his own disk to a Celestial Bow,
Which, higher arched, as lower drops the day-star,
Shall overspan the nations."
                              Joseph bowed,
And glancing round upon the Infant Christ,
Moved on in silence, journeying to the south,
Heart-happy with the hope of glorious things
Which would with gladness fill the universe
Long after his large bones entombed should be.
  The sun had scarcely topped the eastern hills,
Which spread their lengthened shadows o'er the land,
When, passing through old Hebron's northern gate,
They gazed with wonder on that antique town,
Where, full two thousand years before that morn,
The Patriarchs, when the giants were destroyed,
Lived happy lives, and where they left their bones.

One half the town seemed wide awake, the other
Just waking, or still sunk in dreams. They passed
The Pools or Springs, the smaller at the north,
The larger southward. There they paused a time
To mark how up and down its fourfold stairs,
(One staircase at each corner, and each furnished
With one and thirty steps,) the water-carriers,
With many a jocund shout and many a song,
Saluted as they passed and hailed each other.
Stout, brawny men were some, herdsmen, mayhap,
Or camel drivers, sweating under weight
Of water borne in goatskins, (save the legs
The goat complete—strange bottle *we* should think;)
Others, fair, delicate damsels, mostly veiled,
Graceful in motion, springy in their tread,
And all as blithesome as the morning air.
One, with light yoke, on which two buckets hung,
Went tripping down the steps like a gazelle;
Another, gracefully draped and nicely veiled,
As well became an oriental maid
Of modest port, came slowly up the stairs,
On her young head adroitly balancing
A bellying water-jar full to the brim.
This last, beholding Joseph standing there,
Stroking his beard and looking on well pleased,
Stepped timidly up, and bending on one knee,
And holding forth a silver cup, thus spake:
"Good father, thou dost seem a stranger here,
Born, mayhap, far from Judah's mountains; take,
I pray thee, from thy humble handmaid's hand
A cup of cooling water—trifling gift—
Water which Father Abraham of old
Oft tasted in his time—so says the Book—
For which small favor all I ask, my lord,

Is simply thy kind blessing."
Then Joseph took the cup, and raised his hands,
And blessed her once, twice, thrice—then passed the cup
To Mary, who first gave the Child to drink,
Then drank herself, strengthened and doubly pleased:
First, that the water was both cool and good;
And, secondly, because of good old times.
Joseph drank last, and from the self-same cup,
And from the self-same spot those lips· had touched,
Because he was a man of mickle faith,
And thought some hallowed virtue, from such touch,
Might aid the force of that memorial fount.

Joseph's big heart, like green Gerizim's Mount,
Gushed forth with springs of sweetest kindliness,
With no bare Ebal frowning opposite
For curses foul to lodge on. Not because
He hoped the blessing might be blessed to *him ;*
From selfish motives free, he had called down
From heaven a benediction on the maid.
The founts of his benevolence were fed
From veins deep-seated and forever flowing,
Which freshened all around him. But, behold!
What he had least expected came to pass.

Gazing with large-eyed love on Joseph's face,
Behold! the Child has raised his dimpled hands,
And smiling with a smile half arch, half grave,
Such as young cherubs smile in highest heaven,
And prattling on as babes are wont to do,
In half-articulate accents heavenly sweet,
In imitation of his foster-sire,
Behold! with uplift hand and sun-bright eyes,
The whilst on high a sudden rainbow comes
And goes, and haloes play around His head,
HE babbles, lispingly, HIS blessing too.

He blessed his foster-father, then the maid.
Thus *she* received a double benison,
Blessed by the fatherly man, and by the Babe.
Such twofold blessing blessed her through all time:
One, like an unseen chain enwound her heart,
And thence was borne on wings of spirit-dove
Up to God's throne; the other, like a stream
Of heaven-electric fluid flashed adown
The golden links, and thrilled her inmost soul.
  Again the travelers trod the open fields,
And being joined by a stout countryman,
Who owned a farm about a league from town
And now was journeying homewards, much they talked
Of fig trees, olive·yards, and crops of grain,
Of harvest-homes and jolly sheep·shearings.
The man was full of honesty and mirth,
And rattled on in artless, rustic style,
Striving to cheer their way with simple chat.
Good-naturedly the foster-sire joined in,
And asking many questions, answered some.
  "Behold yon terraced vineyards," said the man;
"You should be here, my friend, at vintage-time;
Of all the scenes of mirth that is the merriest.
Then Hebron is deserted; out they pour,
Men, women, young and old, to live in tents
Or booths or summer arbors; music, then,
And dance resound by night and day; young men
And maidens tell each other riddles then,
As Samson used to do in days of old;
For then the world was merrier than now;
Then Roman camps and soldiers were unknown.
I know not how those Romans act at home,
But here they only think of work and war.
Some say the promised Christ shall come ere long

And conquer all the world.   Then Cæsar's men
Must take their flight across the western sea,
And Judah shall be mistress of the world.
But here we part, unless you'll honor me
By tarrying at my farm-house—see it, there,
Bosomed in vines and fig trees—twenty acres—
I have some goats and asses, two fine cows,
An orchard, and a garden, and a wife.
What need of more ?   God speed you on your journey."
So saying, he waved his hand and trudged on home.

CANTO IV.

JOSEPH'S REMINISCENCES OF EARLY LIFE.

" 'TIS well that heaven has given us various tastes,"
   Said Joseph, as the farmer disappeared,
" Else man would ne'er expand his various powers.
With sweat of brow to till the earth for bread,
Though often hard, is not without its charms.
Until my sixteenth year I had been wont
To aid my father in his husbandry;
And oft, from sun to sun, with goad in hand,
Have followed the slow oxen round the field,
Holding the plow, and singing merrily.
   " Once, O how vividly that scene returns!
The morning star yet shone—the sun not yet
Had tipped Judea's mountain-tops with fire
(It was in earliest spring)—when high o'erhead
A flock of wild swans, like a wingéd wedge
In shape, went floating northward.   Far away
They melted in blue space, and their strange song,

So musically wild, so spiritlike,
Grew ever faint and fainter, till it ceased.
  " It ceased, but not the wild emotions which
Upsprung within my bosom—an unrest—
A yearning to roam forth to distant lands.
'And O, for wings,' I cried, 'to bear me on
Buoyant o'er land and sea to the end of the earth!'
The field-flower died that day beneath my plow.
Unheeded; dull henceforth to me appeared
A farmer's life—dull as the clod he treads on.
  " My father read to me the book of Ruth,
And often spoke, in copious discourse,
Of the pure pleasures of a country life,
The ever-varying labors of the year;
How sweet, at dawn of day, to smell the sod
Fresh-turned; how sweet to hear the lowing kine;
How sweet the festive scenes of vintage-time,
The dance, the joys, the songs of harvest-home.
  " In vain; on travel I was bent; but as
Nor wings nor money were at my command,
'I will acquaint me with some useful trade,'
I said, 'and, with my tools upon my back,
Will roam from town to town, from stream to stream,
From the broad western sea to Jordan's flood,
From northern Hamath to the desert sands
That stretch round Kadesh Barnea.'
                          "In short,
With my dear father's hard-obtained consent,
I learned the trade to which I now belong;
And, carrying out my plan of youthful travel,
I traversed far and wide the Promised Land
(The loveliest land beneath the eye of God),
Viewed Bashan's giant cities—standing yet—
Slept on a snow-wreath on the top of Hermon,

And thrice the time the moon doth wax and wane
(Held by the wond'rous witchery of the spot),
On Lebanon's cool top I tarried—lodged
Sometimes in open air beneath the cedars,
Sometimes with shepherds in nomadic tents,
Sometimes with jocund woodcutters, sleeping
In booths at night, and shouting all day long,
With ax in hand, among the cedar trees.
How the green giants crashed beneath our strokes!
Nor did I fail to visit, rapture-smit,
The threefold founts whence Jordan fills his stream.
Swift passed those years of joyous wanderings.

"At last, King Herod, partly to indulge
His love for building, partly to appease
His alienated subjects, Hebrew-born,
Resolved (as *he* said) to *repair*, with pomp,
The second temple, fallen to decay,
But (what was nearer truth) to build anew.
Forthwith full eighteen thousand men 'gan work,
And worked for nine long years without a pause.

"I joined their number. What a busy scene!
From many a land they came; artificers
In wood, in marble, brass, and ivory,
In silver and in gold and precious stones,
From Corinth, Athens, Rome and Persia,
From Asia Minor and Phœnicia,
And not a few from this, our native land.
All cunning workmen here found constant work;
All working on a pattern prearranged,
Which was, as near as altered times allowed,
The pattern given to Moses on the Mount.
Slowly incumbering ruins were removed,
Slowly the solemn edifice was reared.
Unlike the temple built by Solomon,

Which silent, dreamlike, magical, uprose
Without the sound of hammer or of saw,
With Sabbath stillness, seven long, tranquil years;
This came to life with many a painful throe,
With clang of noisy tools, and voice confused
Of many tongues and nations.

                  " Round each stone,
Each marble slab, each cedarn beam, each shaft,
Each tessellated pavement of the courts,
Each portico, each golden gate, my heart
(I wonder at it now, since all is past)
·Was twined with an affection so intense,
It might almost be termed idolatry.
'Tis ever so, I think; the builder's heart
Is wrapt up in the structure which he plans,
Or helps to rear; as that ascends, his soul
Mounts with it, and his eyes behold, at last,
With rapture, the substantial *thing*, which once,
Perhaps long years before, was mere idea.

    " In nine years, then, the fane was fit for use,
Though far from being complete in all details.
In size superior to Solomon's,
It lacked the glory and the sanctity;
Five hallowed things it lacked which had the first—
The Ark, the Holy Fire upon the altar,
The Urim and the Thummim, the Shekinah,
And the prophetic Spirit shrined within.

    " These things I note, lest what I mention now
Might much excite your wonder. One thing more:
Herod, who of the erected pile defrayed
The cost, and by whose order it was reared,
Has striven for years to heathenize the land,
And lacks all reverence for what Moses taught
By inspiration. Herod's god is self;

For selfish ends alone he worships Cæsar,
And to him builds those beauteous marble shrines,
Which, with disgust, I have beheld
Whilst wandering round the land.   One rises near
Fair Paneas, hallowed fount of Jordan's stream;
The other stands in a town by the western sea,
Containing (shameful sight to Hebrew eyes)
Two statues, one of Rome and one of Cæsar.
Nay more, has he not built without, within
Our Holy City, two most curséd piles,
In one of which foul Pagan plays are mouthed;
And in the other—hateful, horrid sight!
Wild beasts, uncaged, are hissed on one another;
And captive gladiators, doomed to death,
Fight till the floor is flooded—grappling now
With lions, now—O! butchery abhorred—
Hacking each other's flesh with blood-red swords?
And then his games quinquennial!—how I hate
The word—and still, not satisfied with these,
He needs must have Olympic games and shows,
Mimes, boxers, dancers, acrobats, buffoons.
O! these things thought of, pain me to the heart,
And almost cause me curse that sanguine fiend,
Possessed by two foul demons, lust and cruelty,
From whom we now are flying.
                    "But, enough;
Words have no power to stay these poisonous woes;
God's power alone can crush them.   To the point:
    "At last those nine long building-years ran round,
And that most gorgeous structure of the world,
Compacted of enormous marble blocks,
With golden spikes high towering o'er the roof,
Stood fit for use (though not yet all complete),
And still some scaffolding incumbered parts

Which needed yet the sculptor's finishing touch
(Chiefly the eastern porch called Solomon's);
When once, at evening's close, I wandered there,
Absorbed in meditations manifold,
Some sad, some glad, all weighty in their scope,
And seized with sudden whim to mount aloft,
I climbed, by aid of ropes and crazy boards,
And stood upon the summit all alone.
Gehenna lay beneath; down, down, down
So deep and black it yawned in shadowy depth,
That Fancy, awe-struck, whispered: ' Mouth of hell;'
And the hoarse winds that moaned along the gorge
Seemed laden with the wails and screams of children
Passing through fire to Moloch.   Owls and bats,
These, circling, 'gan to flit, and those to hoot;
Dogs barked and growled o'er mangled carcasses;
Whilst from a far-off, barren mountain-top
A pack of dolorous jackals, hunger-smit,
Wailed on the muffled ear of coming night,
As if they strove to rouse Abaddon up
T' unsheathe his red death-sword, and let them glut
Their famished maws to the full.   Loud pealed, at times,
Echoing from tower to tower, the watchman's cry;
With clang of bolt and bar the city gates
Were fastened; Kidron's brook, with torrent flood,
Swollen by the recent rain, lifted its voice
Dirgelike, commingled with the sough of pines
And cedars, mourning round the prophets' tombs,
And all things round terrific seemed and dark.
There, on that toppling height I stood alone,
Whilst thought on thought rolled floodlike through my
    brain.
    " My nine years' work was done.   I had been raised
Above all carpenters collected there,
6

And for possession of superior skill
Was called the master-workman. Fir and pine,
Sandal and cedar, olive, shittim-wood,
All costly timbers had been furnished me,
And I had fashioned them to fitting shape
With thoughtful brain and careful hand, forever
Planning, devising, executing, with
Much singleness of purpose, what was needed
For ceiling, floor or wall, for panel-work
Or wainscoting, for ornament or use.
Did I feel proud, and think upon my work
With inward satisfaction? Till that night |
I had done so—until that moment, rather—
But now, a shadow darkened all my soul,
Blacker than that which o'er the Holy City
Was cast by ebon night.
Tears streamed adown my cheeks. 'Jerusalem,'
I cried, 'Jerusalem, how many hearts
Cling to thy walls—thy hills — with love intense,
But chiefly thee, Moriah, highest mount,
Site of God's temple, highest, holiest mount!
To thee, in distant lands, thy wandering sons,
Whether as exiles driven from thee far,
By the great river roaming, or by Nile,
Beneath the shadow of the Pyramids,
Or under terraced Babylon's weeping willows,
Though rivers, mountains, deserts intervened;
To thee, soon as the hour of worship comes,
All eyes, all hearts have ever turned devout,
As though the worshiper believed and felt
That his warm prayers, however winged with faith,
Could never reach the ear of the Almighty,
Unless they rose conjointly with the smoke
Of sacrifice for sin. On thee, 'tis said,

The faithful Father of the promised seed,
With fire and knife and sacrificial wood,
Came with intent to slay his darling Son.
Not far from thee lived Salem's peaceful King,
Priest of the Most High God, Melchisedec;
From yonder mountain's side perhaps he marched
To meet the Patriarch, victorious
From battling with the kings, and rich with spoil;
Not far from thee, perhaps, he offered him
The mystic bread and wine, refreshing food.'
  " These recollections crowded on my mind,
Prelude to thoughts most sorrowful indeed.
'That image of the Godhead, once impressed
Upon man's soul, but now defiled and dimmed,
Say, shall it ne'er be reinstated there ?
The types and shadows of a fiery law
Prefiguring ever better things to come,
O, shall they never—never be fulfilled ?
The blood of goats and lambs and doves and steers,
The morning and the evening sacrifice
Polluting the sweet air with scent of death,
And dyeing Kidron red with streams of gore,
O, when shall all these things be swept away ? '
  " With sobs and tears, with tears and frequent sobs,
I breathed these questions on the ear of night."

CANTO V.

PROSPECTS PAST, PRESENT AND FUTURF.

THEN Joseph thus resumed his narrative:
  " Reflecting thus upon the past and present,
I often asked myself, and asked again:

'These palm-trees, cherubims, and open flowers
Of lily-work and image-work unending,
Carved on the walls, the ceiling, outside, in,
All overlaid with gold of finest hue—
Have all these power, with all their symbolism
Or fancied grace of figures, to wash clean
A soul defiled with sin? O, never, never!
'Twas well, perhaps, and ordered from above,
That these, along with those who used them, should
(As far as the first temple was concerned)
Be borne, as spoils or captures, off to Babylon.
    " 'Sweeter to me than all this wooden pomp,
This wealth metallic, is the tiniest flower
That hides its simple beauty in the grass,
Or peeps with virgin blush from out the rocks.
Yea, e'en the modest lily of the vale,
That masks its spotless bloom in sheathing green,
Teaches and preaches better things to me
Than Solomon, with all his gilded glory.
O, for a church not made with human hands!
O, for a high-priest simple, pure, serene,
To lead us forth into the open fields
Where wheat-stalks, swaying to the gentle breeze,
In graceful undulations bow their heads,
Adoring Him who made them.'
                    "These wild words,
The offspring of the moment, scarce had passed
My lips, before a fear and trembling seized me,
Lest I had uttered something very sinful,
And long I mused in silence. 'Who can tell,'
At last I said, 'but that these images,
These forms symbolic, may prefigure much
Which, though obscure at present, may become,
Under another revelation, clear

As day. As if a man, absorbed in thought,
Eyes fixed on ground, and closely-folded arms,
Should see a shadow floating on before him,
And, lifting up his eyes, should view in air
A strange, large bird, with wide-expanded wings,
Bedecked with starry plumes and golden gloss;
He wonders much from what far land it came,
And oft compares the dark and dusking shade
Which first aroused him, with the wingéd thing
Now gleaming far beneath a rosy cloud.
So, many a dark and dusky type of law
May lead the gazer's wonder-stricken eye
To a reality, sun-bright and clear.
Forgive me, gracious God, if I have said
Aught sinful, or irreverent. I know
How blind is man when light comes not from heaven.
Enlighten, then, my darkness by thy light,
O, lead me forth from this entangled maze.'
After this prayer I stood long sunk in thought,
Revolving many questions hard to solve,
And meditating through the solemn night."
   Here Joseph paused, as if for rest, a time,
When the Madonna, mildly, thus replied:
"What you have said has wakened many thoughts
Which long have slept within me. Listen, then:
Though both of us can trace up our descent
To Solomon and David, for myself,
I ne'er admired the first, nor do I think
Our Holy Book, that mirror of the heart,
E'er holds him up as model to be followed.
Unbounded self-indulgence was his bane.
Sated with pleasure, age came creeping on,
And then life's night to him, instead of stars,
Showed ever-deepening shadows, with the form

Of horned Astarte dimly seen through gloom;
To her he built, on once fair Olivet,
An altar foul, to Chemos and to Milcom,
And sanctioned by his presence—woe the while.—
That fearful spectacle where children passed
Through fire to ruthless Moloch.   Shame, O shame!
He wise?   His actions were nor wise, nor good,
Whate'er his words might be; and such my deep
Aversion to the first, I never could
Nor can admire the second—never—never.
The little good he did soon died away;
The evil seed he sowed took root and throve,
Engendering sin and foul idolatry;
Sin sat beside him on his ivory throne,
Whilst golden lions stood upon the steps;   ·
The very temple which he built to God
Contained the germs of future idol-worship;
The very poem, which some call divine,
However learned Rabbis may expound it,
Searching for mystic meaning in each word,
With animal passion is steeped through and through,
And better suits a worshiper of Thammuz
Or of Sidonian Astarte, than
Him who adores one omnipresent God,
Pure and immaculate beyond all thought.
'Tis this belief of one—one only God,
Which constitutes the glory of our faith;
For this we have been made the chosen seed,
And aught that leads the mind astray from this,
However smooth to touch or fair to sight,
Though fairer than those horses of the sun
Which King Josiah burned in Hinnon's vale,
Should with abomination be beheld,
And with unfaltering hand be swept away."

So spake the Vestal voice behind the veil,
In ever-deepening music to the close.
Joseph, though lion-brave in every nerve,
Had not dared thus to *speak*, though thus he *thought*,
And felt the words thrill through him like a voice
From some far-distant sphere. After due time
He then resumed his former narrative:

"Thus musing, as I said, through half the night,
More tranquil thoughts 'gan roll along my mind,
Like many-colored hoops which children drive
Across some level play-ground. Brighter grew
The prospect, as I mused; at last I called
To memory a passage in Isaiah,
Which brought much consolation to my soul;
And then another from that other seer,
Who, home returned from Babylon, foretold
The building of the second temple. Thus,
Or nearly thus, the inspired words were penned:
And he, full gladly, shall bring forth the headstone,
With shoutings loud, and cries of grace unto it.

"This was the stone on which were graved seven eyes,
The seven high ministers of the Messiah,
Which to and fro do run about the earth
To execute the messages of mercy.
The same rapt seer beheld two golden crowns,
Wherewith to crown the Jesus of that time,
Prefiguring thus the Jesus of *all* times,
The King, the great High-Priest of all the world.

"While thus absorbed and lulled by these grand thoughts,
I fell asleep, and had a wondrous dream,
Which I will tell thee at some future time."

CANTO VI.

UNSEEN THEMSELVES, THEY SEE THE ROMAN CAMP.

MIDWAY between the points of dawn and noon
The ascending sun had journeyed, quaffing up,
The whilst he mounted, from ten thousand cups,
His morning drink of dew; the shadows all
Were slowly shortening; birds, heat-smitten, slunk
Within the wayside copses, having poured
Their early matins forth an hour agone;
And naught of dawning freshness now remained,
Save here and there, beneath some cool recess,
Long spear-grass, jeweled o'er with pearly drops,
Or overshadowed flower-bells, filled with tears,
Wept o'er the grave of morning.
                           Onwards still,
Up hill and down, along a waving land
Like to a wafted vessel sailing south,
The travelers, with undulations soft,
Rose and descended many a gentle swell,
Sweetly conversing as they moved along,
Wrapt in remembrance bland of former scenes,
Or filled with hopes of scenes as yet to come—
When, sudden turning round, they looked—and lo!
An angel walked beside them.
                           Neither knew
How long he there had walked, or how, or when—
And both with pleasure felt a gentle shock
Of quick surprisal. As, some summer day,
After alternate spells of shine and shower,
An unexpected rainbow spans the sky;
We know not whence the apparition came,

Or how the magic arch, so silent-swift,
Was frescoed on heaven's vault—and, wondering much,
We gaze aloft, and thank the Power that sent it.
    At first they knew not 'twas an angel there,
For, like a shepherd lad, with clustering locks
And delicate-tinted cheeks, he seemed to move,
His sheep-hook on his shoulder graceful borne,
And hanging to his belt a pastoral scrip.
Shepherd in outer form and in his garb
He seemed, but from within a lustrous glow
Gleamed ever and anon athwart his limbs,
Like northern lights along the vaulted sky,
Whilst from his eyes a steady radiance streamed,
Like flame of altar-lamps behind the veil.
So bards of early Greece, in fables sweet,
Told how Apollo kept Admetus' flocks,
In guise of youthful herdsman, wandering on
Through vales of Thessaly, with harp in hand;
And how the simple hinds of green hillsides
Were rapture-smitten by his voice and touch;
And how his smothered radiance, ill-concealed,
At times burst forth with Apollonian glow,
And bright flashed forth the Sun-god.
                              On they moved,
The angel stepping soft beside them—soft
As snow-flakes sinking on the grass of spring,
When snow is least expected. On his breast
A bunch of heaven-strange flowers, and on his cap
A wreath of twining stems and colored blooms,
Such as grow not on earth, diffused the smell
Of that far-distant country—strange and far—
Where, with twelve kinds of fruit, the Tree of Life
Waves by a riverside, and every month
Bears a new fruit delightsome. Sandals bright

Buoyed his feet, and ribbons many-hued
And cross-barred bound them to his ankles neat,
And thence ascending midway to the knee,
Ended in tassels gay; each buxom step
He took was like a lifted rainbow small,
And every tread was like the tread of one
Accustomed, when at home, to walk on gold.
"I come," he said, "in search of a stray lamb;"
And, as he spoke, he smiled so archly sweet,
So heavenly innocent, that Mary, too,
Smiled in pure sympathy—smile only seen
By angel's eye, which, through her virgin-veil,
Beheld the rosy smile and rosier blush—
"In search of a stray lamb I come from far;
For eagles are abroad, and a she-wolf
Is hovering round these hills." Again he smiled,
And walked on, silent, by the Virgin's side,
Like one who, having told a riddle, waits
Till time or wit may solve it. The solution
Followed full soon.
                    Before them rose a hill
Dark with o'ershadowing trees, and overlooking
A wide extent of prospect. When they reached
The lofty summit—lo, before them spread
A spacious view extending many a league,
And having in its midst a Roman camp,
Engirt with lofty walls, upon whose top
Armed sentinels were pacing to and fro.
Struck by the sudden sight, the travelers paused
And gazed with deep emotion—almost awe.
"Behold a Roman camp," the angel said,
And pointed to it with his shepherd's staff;
"Behold *one* wheel, one tiny portion of
The vast machine, so cunningly contrived,

So potently compacted, part by part,
Which rolls victorious over land and sea
To subjugate the nations, or to keep
The conquered peoples subject to its rule.
See, further westward, stretching o'er the plain,
The section of a highway, broad and firm,
Raised in the center, sloping at the sides,
And paved with solid stone-work. That strong road,
Built, as would seem, to last forever, leads,
Or will, when finished, lead down to the sea;
And at the water's other verge, another
Of similar construction, speeds to Rome,
Conveying thus her legions to and fro
With most unerring swiftness. Hundred such,
Diverging to all corners of the world,
Spread from the Roman Forum, furnished all
With postal stations and with harnessed steeds
To waft with race-horse speed her mandates stern
To every distant nation crouching round.
  " Behold yon bridge spanning that deep ravine.
If scanned more closely, you would find how firm,
How massive-solid is its masonry,
Though but a slender rill (at times a flood)
Trickles beneath its arch.
                    " 'Tis thus they build.
The same stability marks all they touch.
Their roads, their bridges, aqueducts, their fanes,
Seem fashioned to confront Eternity,
Proclaiming through all time—*a Roman made us.*
And as they build they fight. The same strong hand
With equal skill can wield the sword and spade,
The spear and trowel. And as they fight they frame
Their laws, their treaties, foreign policies,
By force of arms or by diplomacy

Moulding the nations to Rome's iron will.
There's not a soldier in yon bastioned camp
Who says not to himself: 'The Queen I serve
Is named the Eternal—*she* can never fall—
Seven thrones are hers—each throne built on a hill—
And there she sits supreme from age to age,
And ever shall sit, ruling the round earth
As the moon rules the ocean.'   Deeming thus
Himself the servant of such Sovereign Queen,
Whate'er he does with spade, or sword, or word,
Is done as if done for Eternity.
So let it stand—impressed upon the thing,
Whatever it may be—or word, or deed.
   "Such are the people you shall soon behold;
For if you both desire it, I have power
To lead you through yon camp from end to end,
Unseen, invisible to every eye,
And safe as now you stand on this high hill."
   Joseph, delighted, thanked the courteous guide,
And, after consultation held with *her*
Whose will ruled all his actions, said: "Lead on,
We both desire to view the Roman camp,
And have no fear lest any harm or hurt
Assail the Babe, or us, with such a guide;
Lead on; we follow with untrembling steps."
   Midway between the hillside and the camp
The angel paused, and taking from his scrip
What he required for his present needs,
Prepared, by superhuman means, a tent
Or canopy to shield them from the view
Of any mortal eye.   In doing this
He used material means—and thus—as seemed:
A tiny golden box, a crystal vial,
And a thin wand, shaped like a jointed reed—

These were the simple instruments he used.
The wand was formed of several parts, which, fitting
One into the other, swelled, combined, its length
To many feet. It had three subtle springs,
Which, deftly touched, could send forth each a prong;
Each prong of different metal—each unlike
Aught known on earth—each potent to attract
Or to repel. Such was the wand in structure.
Then, from the box he drew a hair-thin chain
(So small its links they scarce were visible),
And hooking one end to the slender wand,
The other in the golden box was coiled.
Next, lifting up the wand arm's-length above
His head, and at the same time deftly touching
One of the springs, a needle-point flew out,
Which drew from heaven, as quick as quickest thought,
A flash electric, which sped down the chain,
And kindled in the box some solid lumps,
Melting them to a fluid. This he poured
Into a vial. Next, with equal speed,
Heating a small-sized diamond to white heat,
He dropped it in the fluid—when, behold!
A vapor issued forth and spread around,
Like volumed wreaths of steam.

                         Then, with his wand
Waving the vapor to what shape he chose
(It seemed obedient to his slightest wish),
Around them and above them, magic-quick,
Uprose a thin rotunda, all of haze,
Arched overhead, and round as that fair fane
Which once by Anio's cataract enshrined
The fire of Vesta, kindled by the sun,
And watched by virgins. Holier fire was here,
Close-guarded by the Virgin of all worlds,

And shrined secure within the rounded space
Of that strange, vapory tent.
                    Unseen themselves
(Such was the nature of that wondrous haze),
They saw all things around them.   As they moved,
It moved with equal pace, and when they paused,
It paused.
            As water, by its nature, can
Assume the form of ice, or wave, or steam,
So, this same substance, wonderful, triform,
Was either solid, liquid, or a gas,
Just as the angel willed.   Now, by his will,
He kept it in the tent-like shape described,
Diaphanous to those within—opaque
To th' outside world, and holding all intact
The veiled Shekinah Glory curtained there.
    And as they moved along, the angel spoke
In simple words, and language plain and clear,
About the Roman army—how enlisted,
Whence named, how organized, and how arranged,
How many troops composed a century,
How many centuries a maniple,
How many maniples a cohort full,
How many cohorts constitute a legion,
How many legions form the force complete,
Stationed in separate camps around the world—
From smaller thus to larger, stretching out
In ever-widening circles.   Thus the mind,
Grasping some object vast and complicate,
Moves on from part to part, from wheel to wheel,
Disjoins, connects, unlinks, and reunites,
Until the whole machine, however huge,
However multiform and many-limbed,
Springs into gear, and plays within the brain,

Filling the soul with rapture. Ne'er before
Had Joseph felt the power of simple words
In all its fullness; words became ideas,
Ideas most living things; and the whole soul,
Enlarging ever as it grew more full,
Rose like a freed balloon, and, soaring up,
Widened the prospect both of earth and sky.
   Scarce had he finished when they reached the camp,
Before whose northern gate, on either side,
A sentinel, in statue-like repose,
Stood at his post, nor looked to right or left,
As though the unvarying sameness of his task
Had hardened flesh and blood to breathless bronze,
And taken away the very power of yawning.
Above the gateway's central arch was seen
A double-visaged Janus. One face looked
In dreamy meditation to the East,
With antique matted beard and eyes half-shut,
Musing on falling empires. Youthful-gay,
With smooth, unrazored chin, the other seemed,
Upward and onward gazing, like to one
Who dreams of Blessèd Islands far away,
And undiscovered Edens in the West.
One mourned, like Saturn, for an Age of Gold
Long since departed; one, with radiant smile,
Saw Golden Ages opening on the view
In beatific visions half-disclosed.
   Unseen, they passed into the martial camp,
Unheard but by themselves they spoke their thoughts,
Unseen, unheard, the infant Prince of Peace
Was borne upon his mother's virgin breast
Among the sons of war.
                    The ground on which
The camp was placed sloped downwards to the south,

Whilst near its narrow entrance rose a knoll,
On whose green swell, o'ershadowed by a tuft
Of palm-trees, was erected, high and cool,
The general's pavilion; conical
In shape, and topped by a bright golden globe—
Type of the world's dominion. Beautiful
In form and color was the canvas structure,
With awning-covered vestibule in front,
Upheld by burnished pikes, whilst, on the sides,
Swords, golden-hilted, crosswise hung for show,
Added their splendor to the martial scene.
Over the whole and in the midmost front
Was seen an eagle, all of massive gold,
Clutching a thunderbolt. Beautiful, too,
On either side the awning of the porch,
A little in advance, uprose the trunk
Of a huge oak, lopped of its spreading boughs,
And tastefully o'erhung with splendent arms,.
All trophy-wise arranged with cunning skill,
Where, gleaming in the sun, appeared to view
A glistening helm a-top;
Spear-heads around the sides, and points of swords;
Hauberks and loricated coats of mail
Around the breast-like center;
Shields, battle-axes, halberts, two-edged blades,
Bows of all kinds and quivers golden-sheathed—
All heaped around in orderly disorder,
As though the work of chance.
                              A day it was
Of high-tide festival for all the camp,
The birth-day of Augustus. Underneath
The awning of the tented porch were seen
Tables containing viands of fine gust,
And rich old wines reserved for gala-days,

At which the general, with many friends,
Was seated, crowned with flowers and ivy-leaves.
Urbane and dignified was all they said,
Manly their port and marked with honest mirth.
A richly-sculptured chalice, of great size,
Was brimmed within with old Falernian wine,
Whilst on the outside, beautiful to see,
Was pictured youthful Ganymede, upborne
By Jove's own eagle, on that jocund morn
Of early May, to be the cupbearer
To high Olympian gods and goddesses.
See, as he mounts, how all his shepherd friends
Gaze wonder-smitten—how the silly sheep
Huddle together—how the 'wildered dogs
Bark upwards!
    Strange that old poetic myths
Like these should still have power to charm us!   Much
The simple-hearted Joseph wondered, too,
What meant such strange translation to the skies,
And first was pleased, but soon was more displeased,
Comparing with the sculptured imagery
Upon the heathen drinking-cup, the pure
Word-pictures he had read so oft
Of Enoch rapt aloft by power divine,
And of Elijah's chariot of fire.
 And then a lyre was brought, and one among
Their number sang a sweet, delicious ode
In praise of him who once was called Octavius—
And of the battle fought at Actium,
And how the peerless Queen of Egypt fled,
And how her lover, deaf to honor's voice,
Fled after her disgraced, debased, undone—
Fled first from battle, then from weary life,
And how the Queen, in all her robes of state

7

Attired, with golden crown upon her head,
In queenly fashion rather chose to die
From poisonous bite of asp, than swell the pomp
Of a proud Roman triumph.   Tears 'gan flow
At these last words; for, more than one there present
Had in their early manhood viewed the Queen,
And knew the wondrous witchery of her charms,
And had beheld her in her gilded barge
Floating adown the Cycnus.   Three times three
Then drank the warriors to Augustus' health,
Dashing the transient teardrop from the cheek,
And fixing swimming eyes on Ganymede,
Until, like him, on fancied eagle-wings
They soared aloft in thought and entered heaven.

  With one consent they turned and faced the south,
When, lo! from that green height the whole wide camp
Was spread before them.   "See," the angel said,
" The streets, how straight; the tents, how regular;
The ramparts, how compact and tall; the moats,
How deep and wide; the whole, how strong and square.
A little city fortified it seems,
Where every man may feel himself secure.
Hark! how those mingled sounds assault the ear,
Shouting of soldiery, neighing of steeds,
The bray of trump, the voice of shrilling pipe,
And all the various din which warriors make
When holiday unchains them.   But, behold
Yon veteran this way moving with slow step,
Surrounded by a group of younger men,
Some slaves, some friends.   That man has made his mark,
And well deserves your study."
                          Nearer, then,
The man came up, and on a seat of turf
He sat him down beneath the fanning leaves

Of a young palm, and thus was heard to speak
Like one who thinks aloud, but little heeding
How those around him may receive his words:

CANTO VII.

VICTOR AND THE EAGLE.

"HO! when will Janus' temple ope again?
When will the thousand bolts be all rolled back,
And War's loud-bellowing voice be heard to roar,
Rousing the drowsy nations into life?
Next month, Mars willing, I'll return to Rome,
And change my war-sword for a pruning-hook,
Working from sun to sun among my vines.
I own a little farm among the hills;
You know the spot—there tumbling Anio roars
In never-ceasing cataracts. The soil
Was once volcanic—earthquakes have been there—
(Best soil for vines) cleaving the mountain cliffs—
The spray of rushing torrents turns to stone
All things that grow around, and every leaf
And every stem seems petrified and hard
As hardest flint. That is the land for me!
And then, what noble views on every side!
The broad Campagna stretching to the verge
Where heaven and earth unite! What aqueducts,
On airy arches proudly marching on,
Convey the waters of the Appenines
Into the very heart of dear old Rome!
Old, and forever young—and beautiful
Beyond all other cities of the earth!
There, cataracts shall lull me into sleep

At night, and into dreams of battle-fields
Long hushed and dried—and in the dead of noon
I'll oft betake me to the temple-porch
Of Vesta, and whilst virgins pure within
Worship the sun-lamp there, which ne'er burns dim,
My task shall be with swimming eyes to gaze
Upon the sun-lit Capitol afar
Till slumber seals their lids.
     "Heigho! these days
Of lazy peace have made a babbler of me.
Time was, my words were few—my red sword spoke—
My tongue wagged little then. 'Tis changed—'tis changed.
It may be I have ta'en a drop too much.
Ho! boys, move round my eagle to the front;
He has not breakfasted to-day. And you,
Ventidius, ope your scrip for meat."

 Then two young men, who bore a littered cage,
Wheeled round and placed it deftly on the ground;
Whereat the grim old warrior lifted up
A curtain, and behold! aroused from sleep,
A golden eagle screamed and stretched his wings.
 "Ha! napping? 'Tis no wonder, brave old friend.
Too long the curtains of thy slumber have
Been closed, shutting dear sunlight out. Again
Thou canst, unwinking, gaze on Phœbus' eye,
And wakened look around thee. E'en the bird
Of Jove, the poets tell us, sometimes droops
His flagging wings, and shuts his fiery eyes,
When the sweet Muses sing. Has sleepy peace
Dulled thy once valiant spirit, noble bird,
Making thee quite forget the mountain crag
Where thou wast born, and whence I stole thee one
Bright summer morn, the whilst thy wingéd parents
Were circling far away in .quest of prey?

My constant playmate hast thou been since then,
And ever shalt be. Thou shalt go with me,
And live again among the Appenines,
And scream among the foaming waterfalls,
The whilst, instead of human limbs, I lop
The limbs of vines, and range my ranks in form
Of quincunx, deeming them my soldiers. Ha!
A merry time we two shall have together.
But come, Ventidius, feel into thy bag,
And give my eagle meat."
Ventidius
Obeyed. The master tossed the meat into
The opened cage, and as the ravenous bird,
With hookéd beak and rending talons, fed
On the raw flesh, and gorged himself full fast,
The veteran soldier, looking on well pleased,
Now grimly smiled, now burst into a laugh,
To mark how well his feathered friend did feast.
Ventidius also laughed, and all the rest.
In sooth, it was a curious spectacle,
To watch by turns the man and the fierce bird,
And note the ways of each.
"A Roman scene,"
The angel said in accents low, but sweet,
Whilst a deep pallor blanched the Virgin's cheek,
And saintly Joseph looked with wonder on,
"A Roman scene, which, painted to the life,
Would make a striking picture. That strange man
Has breathed the breath of contest all his life;
In more than six score battles he has fought;
Full forty wounds (and all received in front)
Might by their scars be traced upon his limbs;
And though he might have risen to high command,
He has from choice remained centurion,

Preferring to be valued for his deeds,
More than for titles and promotions high.
Mark his bold, aquiline nose, his brawny chest,
His strong limbs cast in bronze. Around him stand
Six youths, with pikestaffs void of iron points,
On which are hung, suspended by fine cords,
More than a score of crowns, which he has won
By valor, some for saving life, and some
For spilling blood like water—civic crowns,
Crowns mural, naval—various in their forms—
Of woven oak-bows some, some shaped like towers,
Some like the beaks of ships—all beautiful.
Not only these, but chains of wreathéd gold,
Horse-trapping, golden bracelets, silken flags
(You see them hanging on the pikestaffs), tell
Stronger than language what his deeds have been
In every possible form of soldiering,
By sea and land, on horseback and on foot.
For all his valiant deeds and brave exploits,
The soldiers call him Victor. See, the bird
Has finished his repast, and looks around
Less fiercely. Now, his master opes the cage,
And takes him on his lap and fondles him.
See how he smooths his plumes, and pats his breast,
And gently fingering his haughty neck,
Covers his fiery eyeballs from the light—
All which the proud bird suffers patiently,
For well he knows the hand that feeds him."
                              Then
It happened that among the bystanders
There was a pair of lads, not yet of age
To don the manly toga. They had come
From Rome to Athens to pursue their studies,
And thence, impelled by curiosity,

Had journeyed on to view the far Levant.
They, proud of their supposed proficiency
In the most musical language of the earth,
Kept up a chatting in that heavenly tongue,
Like two young birds in spring. Long robes of white,
Bordered with purple, draped their graceful forms;
Their clustering locks were moist with fragrant oils,
And garlands of verbena crowned their heads.
Now, whilst old Victor, in his mirthful mood,
Was sporting with his feathered playfellow,
Handling his crooked claws and stroking them,
One of the young patricians sauntered up
And laid his girl-soft hand upon the bird;
Whereat the plumy monarch, anger-smit,
With his curved talon struck him such a blow,
That his fine, graceful robe was discomposed,
And a few drops of rich patrician blood
Spotted his snowy garment. Loud the laugh
Which then went circling round the merry group.
Old Victor, with an inward peal of mirth,
Shook through his warrior bulk, and cried aloud:
"A home-made thunderbolt." The lad himself
Blushed—winced—and strove in vain to laugh—
And, heedless now of his sonorous Greek,
Stammered some words in Latin. "By great Jove,"
Said Victor, caging his fierce bird (and as
He fixed the fastenings of the cage's door,
He talked now to himself, now to the bird),
"By Jove, thou hast brought him to his mother-tongue.
Well done, old thunder-dog. Hast scratched him well.
'Twas all because he spoke such pretty words
In Greek. Time was when our forefathers thought
Our native language was quite good enough
To pray the gods with, or to curse our enemies.

Now, our youth flock to Athens. All for words—
For words? Hey! blows are better; not so, pet?"
Then, turning to the lad that had been scratched:
" My friend, you must excuse him for this once.
From beak to claw he is a Roman bird—
And loves the sight of blood. Your hand, Ventidius,
I am not quite as active as I was.
'Tis not so much old age, as that cursed wound
Received upon my thigh at Actium."
    And when Ventidius aided him to rise,
He first was quite unsteady on his legs,
And wreathed like one in pain. " 'Tis over now.
These ancient wounds do sometimes ache afresh,
Reminding us of victories long since won.
Whew! there it comes again, but not so bad.
These twinges make me scream at times—'tis past.
Hark!"—and with sudden start, like one who hears
An unexpected sound, and with curved hand
Behind his ear, much moved, he cried again:
"Hark! to an eagle screaming up in heaven,
Too high for sight, almost too high for ear—
Still, I can hear it faintly."
                        All around
Listened their utmost, but to no effect;
When, lo! the caged-up eagle, with a bound,
Breast-forward plunged against his prison-bars,
Streaming and tearing with his curvate claws,
And gazing upwards, with an eye all fire,
As though he wished to say: " O, let me loose!
O, let me join my kinsman screaming there,
Or I will dash my life out!"
                        Victor wiped
A tear that trickled down his cheek of bronze,
Then, turning to the bearers of the cage,

He said, in tones more mellowed than his wont,
" It was too much for him. The bird is mad.
This is the second time I've seen him thus.
Cover his cage, I say. When in the dark,
He will forget his frenzy. Cover him."
    The boys then drew the curtains o'er the cage,
But still could hear him tossing to and fro,
Frantic and restless still from time to time,
Until the darkness and the prison-bars,
As oft has happened to a man immured,
With the dull pressure of their iron weight,
Cowed down his sky-born spirit.
                              Pause we now
A moment to behold, in swift review,
Some salient points in Victor's martial life.

CANTO VIII.

VICTOR, THE RESCUER.

BORN within ken of the Calabrian coast,
    His boyish days where mainly spent at sea,
Where his rude father was a fisherman.
There, with the changing tides, the tumbling waves
Impart a show of motion to the rocks,
Causing these last to fluctuate to the eye
As though they were astir and animate.
This, in connection with the echoing surf,
Gave birth to many fables. Scylla here,
With all her yelping dogs, was heard to bark,
Opposed to fierce Charybdis.
Here dolphins, seadogs, swordfish, cut the waves
In never-lessening numbers. From the wave

And from the shore his eye might often scan
Ætna, to all appearance poised in air,
Tall, hanging with his white top o'er the haze,
Spouting forth streams of fire. The neighboring shores
Have ever been volcanic. Victor here
Received his first impressions of the world.
Midst earthquakes, whirlpools, lava-floods, and storms,
The muscles of the boy were firmly knit,
And his young eye inured to danger.
                                    Once,
When a dread earthquake shook the aguish land,
And all the villagers fled to the beach,
Embarking (all that could) within their boats,
A loosened mountain tumbled in the sea,
And by its fall raised such a heaven-high wave,
That all on shore, and all in tossing skiffs,
Were swallowed up and lost—he only saved.
A surge had swept him to a towering bluff,
And left him there benumbed, but still alive.
This was his first escape; how many more
He made in after life 'twere hard to tell,
Until at last he looked upon himself
As danger-proof—case-hardened against death.
Early he joined the mighty Cæsar's army,
And was as dear to that great general
As his own eagle is to him. Three times
Has he a Roman rescued from the wave,
Thanks to his early swimming and strong thews,
And still more to his dauntless hardihood.
Once, when a lofty palace was ablaze,
And flames 'gan creep up all the crackling stairs,
He mounted thought-quick to an upper room,
And bore a fainting lady safely thence,
But little scathed himself—she quite unharmed—

A valiant feat, which gained him stores of gold,
Yon civic crown, and richer meed of praise.
    All this, in fewer and in simpler words,
Was told to Joseph by the angelic guide,
Who still was speaking, when a messenger,
With silver wand in hand, was seen approaching
From the pavilion of the general,
And after having bowed with deep respect,
Invited Victor, in the general's name,
To join the merry revelers gathered there.
    He went, accompanied by all his suite,
By all the well-earned laurels of his life,
His crowns, his golden chains, his flags, his scars,
And when he reached the tent, a shout uprang,
Which swallowed all the noises of the camp,
And thrilled the veteran's eagle-heart with joy.
All, standing, drank his health.   Then in the midst,
When he was seated, quick they made him tell
. The story of each civic crown—how won,
What precious life, in winning it, he had saved,
With every circumstance of time and place,
And what the mighty Julius said of it,
And how the mighty Julius looked the while.
    The Angel, as he gazed and listened, smiled,
As smiles some youth of genius, if by chance,
The whilst he treads aspirant up to fame,
He spies beside his pathway boys at play
With top or marbles, shouting loud for joy.
Thus smiling, sweetly then the Angel said:
    "Behold a savior of the warrior-type!
Hark their victorious shouts!   Both for blood spilt
And for blood rescued, they salute him thus,
And do him reverence, even in their cups.
If such an one—half eagle and half man—

Who in his loftiest actions, noblest words,
Still shows some marks of native savagery,
Still, 'neath his golden plumes, displays his talons,
If such an one, for some few dozen saved,
Can win all hearts, all smiles of high and low,
How shall it be when the true Savior comes,
Godlike and Lamblike, to redeem a world?"
   At these soft words the Virgin pressed her Child
With such sweet pressure as young mothers use
When thoughts of coming glories swell their souls.
Such in its kind, but not such in degree,
Her mother-heart, immaculately pure,
Felt the warm heart-beats of the Infant God,
As feels a bud unblown in early spring
The Daystar's pulsing rays, and, inward warmed,
Stores richer odors for the blossoming.
   And now commenced their wandering down the camp;
And soon they reached a spot, where, stored for use,
Stood military engines of all kinds
Then known in war.   Horrid they looked in rest,
Like thunderbolts piled up in sleeping clouds
Before storm-chariots roll.   A shudder ran
Across the Virgin's high-strung, delicate nerves,
When strong imagination, highly wrought,
Made all those monsters live and move before her,
And all the tumult of a town besieged
Rose lifelike into vision.   Now she saw
The catapult discharge its hissing darts,
The huge balista seemed to hurl vast rocks;
Now fire-balls flash, and blazing arrows sweep,
Like falling stars, athwart the gloomy sky;
And still through all, with never-ceasing clash,
Shock after shock, like earthquake, she could hear
The battering-ram at work, and hear the crash

Of tumbling battlements and cloven walls,
And armies tossing in tumultuous fight.
   Between the upper and the lower camp
There was an ample space, where flagstaffs stood
With various banners waving in the breeze;
Banners and ensigns with devices bright,
And fragrant altars garlanded with flowers,
And each alive with sacrificial flame.
At early dawn the ritual had commenced,
And still fat steers and heifers lined the way,
Each waiting patiently its turn to move
Before the reverend pontiff; ruminant
Some stood, as if but half-awake; some lowed;
Some shook their gilded horns as if in sport;
Some pawed the earth, and strove to disarrange
The flowery wreaths and fillets that adorned them.
   With curious eye and meditative mind
Joseph beheld the scene, comparing oft,
And oft contrasting what he now observed
With what he oft had marked on Mount Moriah.
The angel read his soul, and briefly thus
Caused a small tributary stream of thought
To mingle with the current of his mind,
Adding some wavelets more, and tinting it
With somewhat richer colors:
                    "Sacrifice!
How universal round the pious earth!
In peace or war, in happiness or woe,
Man, by the inborn nature of his soul,
Soaring in thought above the present scene,
Looks up to higher powers. The master of
The earth acknowledges a Master o'er
Himself. To Him he consecrates a part
Of what sustains his life—part of the plants—

Part of the animals that own his sway—
Part of the bread—part of the ruddy wine.
Nor is this all the mystery of the rite.
This single act, when comprehended well,
Combines within itself three several acts,
Like a strong braid of three inwoven strands.
By it man strives to thank his God or gods;
By it he strives to expiate his sins;
By it propitiation he would gain.
In these three points the Roman and the Jew
Both think and feel alike; their difference
Consists in this—the Hebrew disbelieves
All other gods but One—Him only serves;
The other builds himself a Pantheon,
Where twelve superior deities abide,
And lesser ones by scores. Another point:
The pious Hebrew ever looks beyond
The present sacrifice, and sees in it
But a faint type of one that is to come,
By whose pure blood mankind shall be redeemed
And all the nations sanctified and saved."
    Whilst thus the angelic messenger discoursed,
The priest, all clothed in robes of spotless white,
Went through an antique ritual, handed down
From the Etruscans and from those that lived
Before the days of pious Numa. First,
He sprinkled on the victim's hirsute front
Frankincense, meal, and salt; next, holding up
A golden vessel filled with choicest wine,
He touched the precious liquid to his lips,
Then poured it out between her gilded horns;
And, lastly, having plucked some tufts of hair
From off her forehead, cast them in the flames
To crackle and consume. And all the while,

Standing in gay clad bands, on either side,
Loud played the harpers, loud the pipers piped;
And loud the snow-white heifer, decked with flowers,
Lowed to her sister heifers not yet slain.
    The victim, then, with all her garlands on,
With all her young life pulsing through her veins,
Was led away to where some butcher-priests
Stood ready, with their instruments of death,
To do the deed of slaughter. Down she fell,
Her life-blood oozing out. Soon, other priests,
With keen inspection, in her entrails pryed
To read therefrom the future.

                        "Pitiful,"
Then said the angel in a mournful tone,
"Most pitiful, that all the fairest things
Of this low world so soon do grow corrupt.
The altars pure, which white religion rears,
Ere long become the dwelling-place of snakes.
The beautiful trees, which piety planted once,
The incense-blossom'd trees, the fragrant-bark'd,
The ever-flowering trees that angels love,
Trees which once waved in Eden ere man's fall,
These all have shrunk and withered long ago,
Part shriveled by foul superstition's breath,
Part girdled (use we here the woodman's phrase)
By cunning priests intent on selfish ends,
Who after cut them down, to build therewith
Abominable altars of false faith!"
    Again commenced their wanderings through the camp;
Some tents they passed where soldiers played at dice,
Or moved their mimic warriors o'er the board.
Their very sports and pastimes smacked of war.
Some were tatooing pictures on their limbs,
Eagles or lions or the beaks of ships;

Here some were pitching quoits, some tossing bars,
There others practiced games of archery;
Some raced; some wrestled; some, with blunted swords,
Were striving who could thrust and parry best;
Some sported with their dogs; some fitted gaffs
To their game-cocks, and urged them on to war.
The scene was ever shifting—ever gay.
   But mark where, in the center of yon square,
Encircled on four sides by warlike tents,
And decked by four times four emblazoned flags,
Two gallant youths, each armed from head to toe,
Are dancing, to the music of a flute,
The antique dance, which, fabling poets tell,
Was framed by Pallas, when the Titan war
Was ended, and she leaped before her sire
In all her ringing panoply superb.
What mazy figures of advance, retreat,
Of onset fierce, and sight-confounding flight,
All regulated by sweet music's dulcet tongue,
As though a cherub, with soft silken cords,
Should hold two ramping lions in his leash,
And, smiling, guide their motions.   Mark the flash
Of gleaming sword-blades quivering high in air,
Like lightning viewed through sunshine. Hark! the clang
And clash of steel on buckler ringing.   On one knee,
Like dying gladiator, now one sinks
As if exhausted, whilst soft flute-notes sob
In pitying requiem o'er him; now erect,
With clamor on they rush, and frantic strokes,
Whilst ever, 'midst the whirlwind and the din
Of combat, modulated forms prevail;
And evolutions shaped by music's power,
And grace of motion, and the charm of rhythm,
Commingle their enchantment.   Beautiful

It was to look upon, and e'en their guide
Smiled with a rosier glow,
And as they turned, thus spake he in sweet words:
"Truly a warlike people see we here.
War colors all they do and all they say.
This purple thread runs through their robe of life,
With red embroidery pictured o'er and o'er.
The Roman bride, preparing for the rites
Of Hymen, has her locks divided
By a sharp spear's point; that she may remember
To what a valiant husband she belongs.
The matron, yearly, on appointed days,
With all her married compeers, keeps a feast
Sacred to Mars, and begs, with votive flowers,
The boon of a brave offspring; and when death
Consigns some noble mother to the urn,
In honor of her well-spent life are held
Funereal games, where swordsmen, with drawn blades,
Fight to the death, and gladiators die."

CANTO IX.

THE EAGLE AND THE DOVE.

AND now, still wandering on, they came anear
The quarter where the cavalry were camped,
And, threading downwards through a narrow street,
Lined on each side with tents, they saw a band
Of horsemen, three abreast, come riding on
Full tilt towards them. Fearful was their speed,
Jocund their shouts, for they were young and gay,
And had been drinking to Augustus' health.
Quicker than thought the angel saw it all,

8

Saw it and formed his plan.   By force of will,
Part of the vapor which encompassed them
Grew solid lightning-swift beneath their feet,
And buoyant bore them upwards.   Up—still up—
They rose so gently smooth and yet so fast,
That the mad horsemen swept beneath their feet,
So that the crystal floor, on which they stood,
Floated aloft, untouched by topmost plume.
    And, ever as they rose, the angel sang;
And, ever as he sang, they higher rose;
And, ever as they higher rose, the camp
Grew smaller in appearance underneath.
    It was a song most low, yet most distinct,
Now, fugue-like, soaring up in chasing notes,
Now lapsing slope-wise downwards—sweet and low,
And all unlike all music heard by men;
For it came thrilling from an angel's heart,
And passed, swift-thrilling, through two human hearts,
And through a third, both human and divine.
And as *it* rose, *they* rose, sank as it sank,
Waving in curves and circles round the sky.
On one side of the camp arose a hill,
On which an oriental plane-tree stood,
Antique and huge in size.   The hollow trunk,
Wide and capacious, could with ease have served
As shelter to a score of living men,
Each man in armor standing by his horse.
Thither the angel lighted with his freight,
So softly that they felt no jolt nor jar;
When straight the magic vapor was transformed
From solid and from gaseous to the form
Of a clear liquid.   This the angel gave,
Encased in a thin golden vial, to
The Blessed Virgin, telling her to keep it
With care about her person.

"A few drops,"
He said, "if sprinkled on the brow or lips
Of man or woman fainting, will revive them.
And in your wanderings over desert sands,
And in the various perils of the way,
Who knows but you may need it."
                 Bowing low,
With graceful inclination of the head,
The Virgin took the vial from the angel,
And gently placed it in a silken bag
Which hung upon her girdle.
               Hark! Above!
A clap of thunder, in a cloudless sky,
Pealing o'er heaven's blue vault! Nor was this all:
Flutter of wings; and lo! a snow-white dove,
Whose plumage had been somewhat discomposed,
Fell downwards from a flying eagle's clutch.
Half-dead it seemed with fright, and somewhat torn
By the fierce war-bird's talons; soon 'twas seen,
With panting heart, to nestle timidly,
Full in the Savior's bosom. With sweet words
Of pity, mixed with dropping tears, He took
The fluttering bird and pressed it to his lips,
And smoothed its ruffled plumage 'gainst his breast,
And wept, and smiled, and kissed it o'er and o'er,
Caressing it with mingled sobs and laughs.
Afar the eagle flew—but ere it sailed
Beyond the scope of vision, sudden grew
The air obscure—another peal was heard—
The light returned—and, lo! the warrior-bird,
As if transfixed by flashing thunderbolt,
Fell from the sky stone-dead. With pointing hand,
Whilst this was passing over head, the angel
Had guided Joseph's and the Virgin's sight,
To view the stricken eagle.

"Lo! a type
Of what shall happen in the after-years!"
And then he took the white dove from the Child,
Although it seemed full loath to leave his grasp,
And, pouring from a vial on his wings
Some drops of a strange perfume he had with him,
He placed the sweet bird in the Virgin's hands,
Who, straightway knowing what the angel meant
Without the use of words, took from her bag
The vessel she had placed there, and began
To sprinkle all its wings, and bill, and eyes,
Until the lovely creature quite revived,
Like thing new-called to life.
                            And all the while
The heaven-sweet perfume scented all the air;
And the bland angel took the immaculate bird
Softly from Mary's hand, and loosing it
With gentle wafture and complacent smile,   .
"Now for the olive-groves," he cried. The bird,
All fresh of wing and sleek in all its plumes,
Upflew the air exultant—circling round
In many an airy wheel above their heads,
The whilst the Child, supine on Mary's lap,
With tiny finger traced its sphery flight,
Describing cycle and elliptic curve,
And moving it as *that* moved in the sky.
But when 'twas wafted downwards, up He rose
Upon his mother's lap and clapped his hands,
And looked towards a distant olive-grove
To which the wingéd Whiteness sailed serene,
Met on its way by half a score of wings,
Some white, some red, some blue, and all sense-charmed
By the aroma that environed it.*

* See note at end of volume.

Within the plane-tree's trunk a loophole large
Had by some idle hand been carved, through which,
Unseen themselves, they could o'erlook the camp,
Behold its stir, and hear its martial din,
A sight well worth the gazing. But, as yet,
They had not tasted food; the heavenly guide
Knew well how much they hungered; then he clapped
His roseate hands, and spake some unknown words,
And straight a table, spread with savory food,
Was wafted down, self-poised. How sweet they feasted,
And with what grateful hearts, need not be told.
Some moderate sips of wine they also quaffed,
Wine pressed from other grapes than those of earth;
It came, the courteous angel told them, from
The sunny vineyards of the Morning Star:
And, as they drank, a feeling of young dawn,
Although the midday heats were on the earth,
Came over them with sweetly freshening coolness.

Finished the feast, they looked again to camp,
And viewed a spectacle of martial pomp,
Such as but seldom meets the eye of one
Who does not follow armies all his life.
It was a mimic battle, all complete,
With van and rear, with middle host, and wings,
With horse and foot, with heavy-armed and light;
Nor wanted waving banner, fluttering plume,
Nor shout of onset, or the clang of trump.
Absorbed, the travelers gazed upon the scene
With breathless interest, and with varying thoughts,
Aye striving, from the mimic show before them,
To realize, in all its vividness,
What war itself must be. At last it closed,
And, looking round—the angel-guide was gone.
Forlorn they felt, at first, as though a friend

Had left them standing in an unknown land
To grope their way alone.   But onwards still
Their impulse urged them; on o'er winding paths
And tracts but little trod; for much they feared
To meet the straggling soldiers on their way.

BOOK II.

BORDERLAND.

CANTO I.

YOUNG ROMAN SOLDIER.

Ultima Cumæi venit jam carminis ætas;
Magnus ab integro sæclorum nascitur ordo.
Jam redit et Virgo, redeunt Saturnia regna;
Jam nova progenies cœlo demittitur alto.

Virgil, Ec. IV.

SIX furlongs distant from the camp, their path
Wound downwards to a deep and shady dell,
Where mossy trees arose on either side,
O'erarching with their boughs a babbling stream,
Which, rippling under roots and o'er rough stones,
Made music sweet and soothing. Turtle-doves
Flew to and fro among the whispering leaves,
And added to the woodland melody
With oft-repeated cooings. An old bridge,
Of rustic structure, stretched from one steep bank
To one as steep upon the other side,
Thus lifting it above the sweep of floods;
And having stood secure for many years,
'Twas covered o'er with moss—antique, but strong—
And offering passage firm to men on foot.
  Midway upon this bridge a young man stood,
With roll of written parchment in his hand,

From which he often read aloud. The youth
Was pale and thin, like one who recently
Had risen from bed of sickness. Large his eyes,
Nose aquiline, hair long and curly. Thus
He stood in meditative mood upon
The bridge, and read and gazed, and gazed and read,
Like one wrapt up in pleasing phantasies.
   Sudden he heard a footstep on the bridge
Approaching, whilst behind him, up the stream,
The splash of hoofs aroused the solitude
Which for long hours had hushed the quiet scene.
Startled he looked around, and wondered much
What travelers these might be, who journeyed thus,
Bound, as it seemed, on some far distant tour.
A manly form he viewed upon the bridge,
And passing o'er the stream a Lady veiled
Was holding in her arms an Infant Child.
With courteous inclination of the head
(Both were brimful of warm benevolence
And of all kindly feelings), they saluted
Each other with all-hails and benisons,
As if each felt that an immortal spirit
(Immortal, though immured in fleshly prison)
Were passing by. Oft Joseph turned his eyes
Towards the beast that bore his treasured loves,
Lest it might slide upon some slippery stone,
Or sink in hungry sands. But, after drinking,
The animal moved slowly, safely on,
And stood, lamb-gentle, on the other side,
Beneath the shelter of a giant oak.
The young man marked his fondly anxious looks,
And knew from the expression of his eyes,
Where then were sphered the loadstars of his life,
Attracting him with more than human love,

And drawing him from self to something dearer.
"Stranger, hast traveled from afar?" he asked.
"From near the Holy City."
                          "Whither bound?"
"To the far land of Nile."
                          "Flying from danger,
Or with intent to visit kinsfolk there?"
"From danger flying—warned by heavenly dream.
I may not tell thee further, youthful friend,
Although thy open looks and kindly eyes
Almost persuade me to relate the whole,
And tell thee many things so new and strange,
As well might task thy faith.   What scroll is that
Thou holdest in thy hand?"
                          "Some written words
We, of the Ausonian land, call poesy;
Thou couldst not understand them, sire, unless
Thou hadst some knowledge of the Latin tongue."
   "That language is to me almost unknown;
But how, being Roman, hast thou learned to speak
The Araméan?"
                          "For two years and more
I lived in Palestine.   My father was
A questor there, and when my mother died,
He still resided in Jerusalem,
And kept me living with him till his death—
Since which I've been a soldier."
                          "Thou dost seem
Like one who has been very ill."
                          "Ay, ill,
Well-nigh to death.   Nine days I was confined,
The last three wrapt in death-like, lethal swoon;
Laid out all ready for the funeral pyre,
When flickering life, which almost seemed extinct,

Returned. I rallied—slowly gained some strength;
But still unable to endure the toil
Of soldiership, I have remained perforce
An idler in the camp.
Of late I have been visiting this glen,
And here have spent some pleasant, thoughtful hours,
Soothed by the coo of doves and voice of streams.
Up yonder, in the hillside, is a cave
To which I oft retire from noonday heat;
Around these hills are winding, shady paths,
And quiet nooks are here, and pulsing founts;
This bridge—yon stream—what more could man desire,
Except some charming work of poesy,
Such as this scroll contains?"
                              He waved the scroll
With graceful curve, and kissed it, showing thus
How much he prized the precious treasure.
                                        Much
Was Joseph pleased to mark the young man's warmth,
His swimming, dreamy eyes and innocent smile,
And the pure marble pallor of his cheek,
As though some work of sculpture had ta'en life,
And the fine chiseled stone were animate,
And now held parley with him. Oft it seemed
As though a spirit on that rustic bridge
Were standing near him—some pale visitant
From death's mysterious realm, with scroll in hand,
Containing notice of an unknown world
Beyond the grave. Again he questioned him
In gentle words:
              "The poet's name, I pray thee,
Inform me, and the subject of the writing?"
  "Virgilius was his name—Virgilius Maro.
His father was a farmer, and their farm

Was on the river Mincius, near to Mantua.
There was the poet born—I've seen the spot.
My father also owned a farm hard by
Which much resembled it—fine pasture-land,
Sloping down to the water-side—behind
Were craggy rocks, fit haunt for climbing goats.
Around the homestead beach-trees stood, and elms
O'ercanopied with vines; and in the garden,
Through which a tiny brooklet wound, was seen
Rich store of beehives, ever humming sweet,
And lulling you to slumber. Wood-pigeons
Kept up a gentle cooing on the tree-tops;
And there the poet spent his early boyhood."
    "A fitting birthplace for a poet," said
Joseph, in answer. "Was he prophet, too?"
    " He called himself a prophet," spoke the youth,
" As prophet most men look upon him now.
This roll contains his Pastorals—so called;
And one of these, addressed to Pollio,
I was engaged in reading when you came.
I wish, sire, you could read it for yourself.
Some say 'tis based upon a prophecy,
Which, six long centuries ago, was sung
By the Cumæan Sibyl in her cave,
In which is mention made, in mystic verse,
Of what shall happen in the aftertime:
Of an Immaculate Virgin, who shall be
The Mother of a Godlike Child divine,
And of a second happy Age of Gold;
The lion then shall lie down with the lamb;
The child shall sport uninjured with the asp;
The fields shall yield spontaneous crops of grain;
Sweet flowers shall spring where brambles grew before;
Dread war shall cease, and universal peace

Bless all the nations all around the earth.
Sometimes I think that happy time will soon
Burst on the world. E'en now, e'en now, methinks
Some signs proclaim its advent; how my heart
Dances with rapture at the thrilling thought!"
    And, as he spoke, his sickly cheek was tinged
With a slight, delicate rose of faintest red,
Which some would have pronounced the rose which Death
Oft paints on cheeks he marks to be his own.
    Joseph was deeply moved. Was it not strange,
He thought (and, thinking, stranger still it seemed),
That a far Pagan poet should write thus;
Should weave in Latin verse the self-same thoughts,
The same ideal types and images
Used by inspired Isaiah?
And who, then, could those mystic Sibyls be,
Of whom he had heard mention more than once,
But always dimly, vaguely? More than one,
'Twas said, had lived and prophesied on earth,
In Europe and in Asia. Even then
('T was faintly whispered) one of these still lived
In a secluded valley, locked and barred
From all the world by gates of solid rock,
And that her songs still breathed of truth and life,
Though centuries had passed by since her birth.
These thoughts came crowding on his mind, the whilst
That young man, scroll in hand, before him stood
Upon the bridge, wrapt in a waking dream.
Then, beckoning him to follow, on he passed,
And walked towards the jewels of his soul.
    Startled by hearing footsteps coming near,
Mary turned round her holy head to look,
When—quick as thought—the Roman caught a glimpse
Of the most heavenly human face that e'er

Imagination pictured to itself
In moments of the deepest ecstasy.
'T was but a moment's vision.   Instantly
Her back alone was seen; she fixed her veil,
And when she turned again, her face was hid,
Hidden the curve of neck, the arch of brow,
The sweet and innocent mouth, the dimpled chin,
And, O, those eyes! all—all were masked from view;
For, though the eyes could still be dimly seen,
Like overclouded stars, their holy rays
Were quite obscured and dimmed.   The pallid youth,
Slow sauntering by the man of middle age,
Came up in wondering admiration wrapt,
And finding thus the mother's face concealed,
Gazed, spell-bound, on the Child.
                              O, who can tell
What a sweet influence, never felt before,
Those holy Infant eyes cast on his soul!
Like consecrated altar-lamps, were they
All filled with holiest oil?   O, no, no, no.
Too tame, too tame!   Small planetary orbs,
Reflecting radiance from a hidden sun
And beaming on the world with all the power
Which old astrologers once dreamed about?
Too weak, too faint!   Sun-rays from drops of dew
In summer morn reflected, when fair flowers
And blossoming branches wave within the breeze?
All too inadequate, too faint, too dim!
    Could this, then, be the Infant Wonderful,
Of whom he had been reading on the bridge,
The Virgin Mother this, so long foretold
By mystic Sibyls living far apart,
Foretold by Hebrew prophets, holy men
(For he had heard some rumors of their works),

And was the Golden Age about to dawn,
Which the great Mantuan poet had foresung?
Had not the peopled earth itself become
Prophetic through the continents and isles?
Were not strange voices borne upon the winds,
And strange oracular meteors seen at night?

As when an arm of the sea, which winds far up
Among the lonely hills, at time of flood,
Sucks up the tidal wave through all its turns,
And swells and pants, and fluctuates with the heavings
Of the huge ocean-heart of all the world,
Thus through that young man's soul went billowing
The spiritual influences then
Abroad among the nations of the earth.
The flow of his emotions was too high
For his weak health to bear.   First overstrong
He felt through all his nerves and fibers—then
Weak and aye weaker—till at last he fell,
Like one bereft of life, upon the ground,
And lay all motionless in a deep swoon.

Following the promptings of her woman's heart,
Mary, the Blessed One, dismounted quick,
And throwing óff her cumb'rous veil, began
To chafe his wrists and temples; all in vain.
He moved not—showed no signs of quickening life.
She then bethought her of the vial, which
The angelic guide had given her, that same day;
And how 't had cured the dove, which, sooth to say,
Looked not more innocent or whiter than
The youth who lay before her motionless.

Like raindrops from the sky, after long drouth,
Upon some lovely flower which droops to death,
The magic liquid exercised its charm;
Then Blessed Mary raised her hands in prayer—

Her hands—her eyes—and eke her dulcet voice,
And begged the Father, Son, and Holy Ghost,
To save the young man's life, and raise him up
From his death-swoon, and grant him health again.
  Her prayers and angel-sprinklings did their work.
Soon, those large eyes, like planetary stars,
When clouds which hid them have been swept away,
'Gan shine with deepening luster. First, from far
Their beams appeared to radiate—far away—
From some high silvery sphere beyond the earth,
As if their light, in journeying endless space,
Had not yet reached in full this nether globe,
So little recognition did they show.
But soon their human beaming came to them;
And when he was aware that the sweet face,
Which hung above him then so heavenly fair,
Was the same lovely visage he had seen
When walking from the bridge, his first impulse
Was to adore and worship. But he scarce
Had uttered half a sentence, ere her brow,
Before so sweetly arched, grew blandly stern;
And thus she spake, in accents finely tuned:
  " Worship not me, young man, I humbly pray thee;
I am a human being like thyself;
Like thine, my body shall one day become
The food of worms; worship not me; I am
A passive instrument in Higher Hands;
A simple handmaiden before my God.
That Infant thou seest sporting on the ground,
With butterflies around him, seems to me,
Deep musing on the mysteries of heaven
(Mysteries too vast for human mind to grasp),
A blessed dewdrop, through whose tiny orb
God-sunbeams are refracted. HE who made

Both sun and dewdrop, lives in that small CHILD,
He *is* that CHILD—pervades unbounded space—
Is ever omnipresent—made all worlds—
And still upholds them—see HIM sporting there—
HIM thou mayest worship; more I dare not say.
Farewell. Tell no man what thou hast beheld
To-day, for worse than bloodhounds are unleashed,
Coursing o'er hill and valley, field and town,
Athirst for infant blood. With God I leave thee;
Thy health, I'm sure, will be much better now;
Conform to nature; get thee wife and child;
Brood not too much on fathomless mysteries;
Fulfill the daily duties of thy life,
Wherever these may lie, in camp or town,
Or country—ever faithful, ever true—
So God, in time, may take thee to Himself,
And we may meet thee in a better world."

Thus speaking, with a calmly pitying smile,
Again she slowly fixed her wonted veil,
Most womanlike in every act and speech,
A woman of the purest, loveliest type,
Without one touch of artifice or pride
Or affectation; all her winsome ways,
And all her graces, seemed pure gifts of heaven.

And when she had resumed her wonted seat,
The foster-father lifted up the Child
With softest care, and placed him in her lap,
Arranging everything as was most fit
For travel. Then the young man to the Child
Bowed reverently, and said a fervent prayer,
And kissed the young Child's feet once—twice—yea,
    thrice,
And then saluted him who watched the Child,
And three times decorously waved his hand

To her who bore the God-child on her lap,
Then slowly loitered bridgeward, often turning
To view the Holy Family on its flight.
    From that day forth that young man's health grew sound,
All tendency to swooning disappeared;
And though he was a faithful Roman soldier,
He was at heart a guileless Christian too.
Some say he was that good centurion,
Whose servant, sick to death, in after days,
Was cured by Christ, our ever-blessed Lord,
Because the servant's master had such faith.

CANTO II.

HUNTERS' RENDEZVOUS.

THEN, as in wonted wise they journeyed on,
  The Blessed Virgin thus expressed her thoughts
To him who walked beside her:
              "What I did
Before we left the Roman youth, might seem,
To some, indecorous and contrary
To the established customs of our land.
If *thou* dost think so, tell me plainly now,
That I in future may be more on guard."
    Then answered Joseph promptly: " Spotless one,
What thou didst to the young man in his swoon,
Both at the time, and now that it is done,
Seemed, and now seems to me, the stainless act
Of warm benevolence and charity,
Acting from purest motives. Just as soon
Would I cast blame upon the silver moon,
Who oft at night, as if in pity, throws aside

9

Her veil of cloud to aid some wayfarer,
Belated in the woods, and foot-weary,
And almost dead with toil."
                    " It gives me joy,"
Answered the Virgin, " thus to hear thee speak.
I am no prophetess, but I believe
(I scarce know why or wherefore) that the days
Are coming, when, in other lands,
More to the westward, woman shall be deemed
Man's helpmate and companion, not his slave.
Like earth and moon, each in its separate sphere,
Shall man and woman, with fair offices
Of mutual good, but different in kind,
Help and irradiate other—both, and each,
Reflecting light drawn from a mightier power;
And each, to make the other's course more bright,
Turning to view the God-enlightened side,
Which, th' other seeing, may believe that God,
Thus smiling on the sky-companion, smiles
On *him* or *her*.   Perhaps I have not made
My meaning plain—but I believe the days
Are coming, when *one* shall mate with *one*, like doves,
Communing thus by pairs, by loving *twos*,
To form the *third*, the children of their love,
And all combined in trinal unity,
For succor, comfort, solace, and delight.
Then shall our cumbrous veils and harem walls
Be swept away like things beyond the flood;
Then inward purity and innocent thoughts
Shall shine translucent through the unveiled face,
Making companionship between the sexes
Free, guileless, and delicious."
                        Joseph smiled,
And gently wiped away an oozing tear,

So dewy-fresh and new her thoughts appeared
To him, who, though an oriental born,
Was ever hoping for a better world;
And, as he listened to her musical words,
E'en then he seemed within it.   Novelty,
With purity and innocence combined,
Fresh-bursting ever from that virgin spring,
Watered his manly soul, and kept it green
And flowery forever.
                                    On they went,
By any road or footpath, found by chance,
Which seemed to lead south-east.   The shadows, by
Their length and their direction, served as guides,
Both as to time and bearing.   Ever wilder
Stretched a rough, savage country on before them,
With mountain piled on mountain, towering high.
For miles they moved in perfect solitude,
Or only passed some scattered mountaineers
Or goatherds, seated in the shade, the whilst
Their flocks hung browsing on the rocks.   At last,
They saw below them, in a mountain vale,
A spectacle, which, suddenly beheld,
Excited much of interest, some of dread.
A rendezvous of hunters it appeared,
Who, by their aspect and apparel, seemed
A band of Roman soldiers.   Fair the scene
And beautiful to view it was, in sooth:
An emerald meadow, watered by a stream,
And cooled by fanning trees, stretched under cliffs,
Which, rising high and rugged, fenced it round
On all its sides, save two.   Through these the stream
Flowed in and out with graceful curving bends,
Accompanied by ever-freshening airs,
Which, sporting with the foliage and the flags,

Imparted gayety to all around.
A fountain gushing from a rock was seen
On one side, and round this was grouped a score
Or more of jolly huntsmen, in all attitudes
Of frolic or repose—some half-asleep
In the long grass; some drinking with loud shouts;
Some cooling in the fount their wine-flagons;
Some dancing with a bevy of wild girls,
Perhaps descendants of the Moabites.
　　About a bowshot from the revelers
Others were gathered round an open fire,
With hooks and forks and pans and butcher-knives,
Cooking the various game—a busy scene.
Hove then in sight another company,
Through the north valley-entrance suddenly,
Bearing along, as products of their sport,
A stag with branching antlers, a wild swine,
A swan or two, and other smaller game,
All piled upon a broad-wheeled creaking wain,
Drawn by two milk-white oxen. Dogs before
And dogs behind; some with long sweeping ears,
And some with ears erect, came trooping round.
These hunters also had gay maidens with them,
Picked up among the hills and valleys round;
Some dragged unwilling from their tents and huts,
But most of them, by voluntary act,
Following the soldiers when the hunt was done.
Half-bacchanal, half-sylvan was the group,
Composed of men and women, boys and dogs;
Some rode on mules, and some on dromedaries;
On asses some, and some crept slow on foot.
With shouts and pæans, those around the fount
Saluted the new-comers; meeting them
With cans and flasks brimful and nicely cooled,

And begging them to drink, and drown all care,
For this was Cæsar's birth-day.
                                    Louder soon
And more tumultuous grew their boisterous mirth,
Gayer the song and livelier the dance;
The women, like Bacchanti, tossed in air
Their uplift arms, and loosed their waving locks,
Tripping along in tipsy jollity,
Wine-cup in hand, and madness on the brain,
All crying: "Long live Cæsar."
    The path, which led the holy travelers on,
Wound round the brow of one of the steep heights
Which walled the valley in upon the left,
And, as they moved, they saw the drunken scene
In all its shifting frenzy. Mary, then,
Pained through her inmost being, cried: "O, haste,
Hasten to leave this loathsome spectacle,
Which shows how low humanity may sink
When decency and virtue lose their sway.
The very air seems foul with unclean spirits,
And though the world is all ablaze with light,
I feel like one who treads a dreary path
At night, when all the sky is black, and winds
Are howling—haste, lest evil demons come
And plunge us down the cliffs."
                                    Then Joseph led,
With sturdy hand and step, the beast along,
Hoping to pass unseen by those below,
And so escape their notice. 'Twas not so;
Upon the mead a group of stalwart men
Were practicing, just then, at archery,
Not quite a bowshot distant; one of these
(Of coarse and satyr visage was the man,
Full of lewd jests and loathsome thoughts obscene,

Half-drunk to boot), having caught sight of them,
With brutal oath, and foul, Silenus-sneer,
Discharged an arrow from his bended bow
Full at the Virgin Mother and her Son.
　·Whizzing the arrow sped—but, ere it reached
The mark intended. sudden from its path
It was diverted by some unseen power,
And fell all harmless on the ground behind them
Some sixty paces off.　The man turned pale,
For he, as Roman soldiers always were,
Was coarsely superstitious, weakly so,
And knowing what a demon housed in his heart,
Thought himself thwarted by some potent spirit,
Some genius of good, which, in the end,
Might work him woe.　Down fell his bow, unstrung—
He tried to laugh, but laugh he could not—a
Sardonic grin convulsed his ugly face,
And, to avoid the sight of his compeers,
He wandered·to the woods, like one possessed.

CANTO III.

"PAN IS DEAD."

ONWARDS and upwards, then, the travelers passed
　Along a wilderness of mountain land,
Height after height ascending.　Every step
The way grew wilder and more desolate.
The very pines and cedars shrunk to dwarfs
With stunted stems, and crooked, twisted boughs,
And snake-like creeping roots, that strove to catch
And trip the feet of those who passed that way.

Higher and higher still! At last they reached
A spot, which seemed the loftiest of all
The neighbor eminences; hushed as death
It stood beneath a sky of darkest blue,
Unvisited by any sound of man
Or beast or bird. Far off, in distance dim, .
A little west of north, appeared to view
Jerusalem's temple, stationed on its height,
Now vanishing to nothing; further east
The Dead Sea glimmered faintly in the sun,
With Abarim beyond it, peak behind peak;
Southward, far stretching, like a distant sea,
The desert faded into scarce-seen blue;
Mount Hor was visible, but barely so;
Whilst nearer, and beneath them, ridges wild,
Needles of rock, and jutting mountain-horns,
Rose in chaotic grouping all around,
With here and there a black, deep mountain glen,
Which seemed to cleave earth's center. Moments few
The travelers passed in silence on that spot,
Feeling as if cut off from all the world,
Severed from human kind and voice of life,
And were about to journey on, when, lo!
The flap of distant wings—but not of birds—
The sound of distant song—but not of men—
Arresting their attention, made them pause.
Another momentary silence hushed
As death! and then a sudden symphony
Of instruments celestial! Then was heard,
Sung by angelic voices, a sweet hymn,
Which words of mine can faintly shadow forth,
But which, in substance, sounded somewhat thus:

HYMN OF THE ANGELS TO THE BLESSED VIRGIN.

Ave Maria!
From pole to equator
Through every latitude,
With praise and with gratitude,
In full-souled beatitude,
Mankind shall sing to thee:
Ave Maria!
Spotted Sin (how we hate her),
Cloven Pan and each Satyr
Have fled, have fled.
O'er land and o'er ocean,
In all its vastity,
The whole world shall ring to thee;
Dove-eyed Love and Devotion,
And white-pinioned Chastity,
And high-toned Emotion,
Tenderly fluttering, sweet pæans uttering,
Is each on the wing—on the wing to thee.
Ave Maria!
O'er the isles, o'er the continents,
Voices sweet are heard singing now,
" They have fled, they have fled;"
A mystic cry (hark!) is heard ringing now,
Heard by shepherds and fishermen:
" Pan is dead—Pan is dead;"
Echoing, echoing,
Ever re-echoéd,
" Pan is dead,
Pan is dead."
Ave Maria.

Joseph, though little skilled in Grecian myths,
Yet comprehended quick the mystic words
Echoing above, below, and all around,

And knew within his heart that they announced
The downfall of all soul-corrupting creeds
Then dominant in Greece and Italy,
Those master nations of the ancient world.
Thanks to Jehovah, the Almighty One,
These all were down-fallen now—down-stricken—dead.
   And strange! those same mysterious words, 'tis said,
Were heard years after by a fisherman,
Lone rocking in his solitary boat
In the Ionian sea, when—"*Pan is dead,*"
Came swooning from afar across the waves,
Re-echoed by the Acarnanian shore
And the Echinean isles—"Great Pan is dead;"
Rumor of which soon after having reached
The ears of lewd Tiberias, all his court,
All his astrologers and soothsayers,
Unable to interpret what they meant,
Were stricken pale with fear.
               The greatest joy
They brought to Joseph, who straightway announced
Their meaning to the Lady by his side,
Who likewise testified her heartfelt rapture.
Then, after prayer upon that mountain-top,
They 'gan descend full swiftly, for his eye,
Well skilled in weather-prophecy, had marked
A slender bank of cloud far to the west,
Which seemed but newly risen from the sea,
And which, he thought, attracted by the mountains,
Would sweep to eastward, burst upon their peaks,
And end in sudden tempest. Down they sped,
Rapid as their sure-footed beast could tread,
Following the slender pathway over rocks,
And rough ravines, and forests of dwarf pines,
Mostly in silence, for the need was great,

And great the skill required of hand and foot.
Thus passed almost an hour; at last they reached
A lower range of mountains, not so dead,
But clad with lofty pines and evergreens,
And freshened by the spray of waterfalls,
And here and there enlivened by the voice
And wing of bird.
    But lo! o'erhead the clouds
Are gathering fearfully; a prelude low,
Of muttering thunder, seems to growl—"Make speed
To find quick shelter, or ye may be lost;"
The winds, before asleep, fierce waken now,
And, sounding awfully among the pines,
In unison with thunder, seem to chant:
"Make haste—seek shelter quick—ye may be lost."

CANTO IV.

THE CAVE OF SEVEN CEDARS.

THREE bowshots o'er a space all bare of trees
They passed with rapid footfall, when, behold,
A cavern's opening mouth, a sheltering cave!
Cave of the Seven Cedars it was called.
On either side three cedars, one on top;
All fine and noble trunks, like those that grow
On Lebanon. Then Joseph, peeping in
The grotto's opening, found that it was dim,
Dimmer than evening twilight when all glow
Has left the horizon, and black night creeps on;
So straightway he alit in haste a torch,
Which he, before the journey, had prepared
With nicest care, and kept within a sack

Slung o'er the beast, with tinder-box and flint
All ready for quick use. The torch was soon
In blaze, and soon its beams displayed to view
A spacious cavern, snug and dry and warm,
Which seemed to open into other rooms
Reaching far inward.

     With a gradual slope
The subterranean floor went shelving up,
So that the coming floods, however fierce,
Could find no access there. A limpid stream,
Whose fountain-head was deep within the mount,
With even pulse came lapsing down the rock,
Unquickened by the hurricane without,
Which even now had fallen upon the woods,
Clashing their tops and tearing up their roots
With an earth-rending clamor. Scarce a breeze,
Scarce a side-eddy entered the cave's mouth,
So firmly on each side 'twas buttressed round
With rocky ramparts, shielding it from winds
Which swept, wild blustering, from the opposite point.
There all was calm within. A fervid prayer,
Spontaneous, heart-outgushing, snowy-winged,
Flew through the tempest up to God's abode, ,
And, as it glided through the golden gates,
The angels fanned it on its fragrant way,
And seraphs swung their censers to and fro,
To waft it onwards to the Father's throne,
Enwrapt in sweetest perfume.

       Joseph then
Helped the Immaculate Lady to dismount,
And, spreading on the cavern's floor a soft
And bright embroidered carpet, in whose woof
A palm-tree was impictured and a pair
Of white-winged doves, of woven work superb,

He bade her rest in peace, whilst he himself,
Fixing his flambeau in the fissured rock,
So that its glare might not offend her eyes,
Drew from his pouch a nicely-written scroll
Of well-preserved papyrus, and began
To intone its holy scripture.

                   O, how grand
That antique language of the earliest world,
Whose every word was like a thing alive,
Instinct with many meanings, flashing out
Like lightning from Jehovah's chariot-wheels,
And, as it passed into the listener's brain,
Arousing there old echoes which once pealed
Among the hills of God—how grand and full
It sounded through that cave—from manliest lips
Outpouring like a jubilant mountain stream
Full fed from heaven-filled waters! How each pause,
Each cadenced ending, grandly was attuned,
And made still more sonorous by the plash
Of million-pattering raindrops heard from far,
And furious, wailing winds, and tumbling cliffs,
And floods down-roaring to the dread abysm,
And all the crash and turmoil of the storm.
And ever rose, through all, "the still, small voice,"
Which, tremulous and plaintive, oft did sound
From out the reader's inmost heart, which mixed
With all, and formed the base of all, with overflow
Of saintly tears soft trickling down his cheeks,
And dripping on the holy page like dew.

   His lectern was a shelf of caverned rock;
His sounding-board the grotto's fretted vault;
His hassock rugged stone; his light a torch
Such as a traveler fires in greatest haste,
When storm and darkness, furious rushing on,

Threaten to swallow him up; his listeners
A Holy Virgin and more Holy Babe;
The winds and waters loud his choristers,
Answering each other in alternate stave;
His Book the oldest, holiest in the world.
   And such a reader! Few, we know, read well.
With him it was an inborn, heavenly gift.
The whole man read; tongue, teeth, throat, palate, lips,
But chiefly heart and brain; the volumed sound,
In rhythmic sequence following wave on wave,
Made up a musical current so complete,
So tunable and grateful to the ear,
That she who listened found herself enwrapt,
Both soothed and stirred, excited and composed;
Each word, each syllable, each letter even,
Became alive, and told its own sweet tale.
For manly strength combined with fluent ease,
For compass and expressiveness of tone,
For sweetness and for force, his reading might
Be likened to that wondrous water-organ
Renowned of old in Alexandria,
Which a keen, subtle-thoughted brain devised,
And hung in Zephyr's temple; by strange art,
Currents of air by water's force were driven
Through delicatest tubes, now strong, now soft,
So cunningly contrived, so nicely fashioned,
That when the music played, it seemed as though
The lofty dome were mounting in mid-air,
To yield a prospect of that loftier one
Reared by the world's great Author; so it seemed;
And many a traveler, many a pilgrim felt
The melody's enchantment. Thus it was
With Joseph's wonderful reading.*

           * See note.

                    Wrapt away
In fancy to the times beyond the flood,
And lulled into a sweet, poetic dream,
Not quite asleep as yet, nor quite awake,
The Virgin gently sank into a state
Of pleasing languor, full of phantasy,
Like some sweet bird upon a rocking bough,
After the time of sunset. Deeper down
Into the realms of slumber soon she lapsed,
And soon her beautiful eyelids veiled her eyes
As sunshine veils the stars. Much had she seen,
And much was still to see ere close of day,
And nature needed some repose and rest
After so much excitement. By her side
The Almighty Infant slept as sweet a sleep
As did the roseate mother.
                     Still the storm
Outside swept furious o'er the mountain-tops,
And still the pious reader, wrapt, absorbed,
With eyes fixed on the old papyrus scroll,
Aroused the dead words on the antique page,
Making them start to life and melody.
Turning his head at last, he bent his view
Towards the load-stars of his life. Behold
A sight of terror!
Behold a monstrous lion crouching there,
As if in act to spring. Yea, near the feet
Of the two sleepers! Flying from the storm,
The savage beast had sought a shelter there,
His tameless nature tamed and quite subdued
By all-resistless thunder. Still he lay;
Perhaps he meant not, couchant though he was,
To make the fateful spring; quite cowed he looked,
And overmastered by some potent spell

Which made him like a sculptured lion seem.
Then Joseph, on the instant, seized his torch,
And, moving towards the monarch of the woods,
Full in his eyes he shook the bickering flame,
And roused him from his catlike attitude.
One moment man and beast glared at each other—
The next—the lion wheeled and fled the cave,
Swift-rushing forth into the maddening storm,
And howling down the mountains. Hark his roar,
Mixed with the thunder's voice and din of floods!
   Whilst all this passed, the Holy Lady slept,
Still slept the God-born Child. In sweetest dreams
She, slumber-bound, was holding converse high
With seraphims and bright, cherubic shapes,
'Midst heavenly plants embowered, beside a stream
In Paradise, with harpers harping round—
Sleep within sleep involved, dream wrapped in dream.

CANTO V.

RENDEZVOUS OF ANGELS.

HARK, from the far back chambers of the cave,
   The sound of harp and dulcimer and lyre
Mixed with angelic voices floating on,
And momently approaching! On they came,
And soon appeared in view, as if upsprung
From the old mountain's inmost heart; with smiles
And nods they moved before the saintly man,
With smiles and waving hands; fair garlands hung
Above their arching brows; with rhythmic step,
Half dance, half leap, with graceful speed they tripped,
And when they reached the spot where slept the Babe,

All dropped with one accord on bended knee,
And scattered roses, yellow, white, and red,
In handfuls at his feet. Then, through the cave's
Rock-guarded mouth they floated gleeful forth,
Aye sweetlier chanting.
                Hark! another band
Above the clouds make answer! List their song!
As though the place and hour had been prefixed
By mutual appointment there to meet.
That moment, the erst furious storm grew calm;
Outburst the westering sun; far rolled away
The thunder o'er the distant mountain-peaks;
Hushed grew the winds; God's rainbow spanned the east;
Ten thousand raindrops sparkled on the trees,
And of the passed-by tempest naught remained
But prostrate trunks and toppled, upturned crags,
And loud-voiced torrents tumbling cascade-wise
From rock to rock.
   "Hosanna to the Lord," rang from the sky;
"Hosanna to the Lord," from the cave's mouth
Resounded. Joseph then, with gentlest touch,
Wakened the Virgin, chanting, with low voice:
"Arise, arise! the tempest's voice has ceased;
Angels are waiting at the cavern's mouth;
Angels are coming from above the clouds;
The rainbow's arch is spanning all the east;
The westering sun in pomp will set ere long;
Arise, come forth, sweet Mother of the Lord,
Lady Immaculate! Come forth and see
The splendor, and the beauty and the glow,
Now doubly pleasing after all the toil
Of our long wandering through the Roman camp,
And o'er the barren mountains beat by storms."
   The Virgin Mother opened soft her eyes,

And smiled, and rose, and lifted up the Child.
Then Joseph quickly quenched the burning torch,
Unjointed it, and placed it in the sack,
With flint and tinder-box, for future use;
Relieved the Mother of the Holy Weight
That rested in her arms, and soon the pair
Stood calmly gazing near the cavern's mouth,
He, of ripe middle age, but blooming fresh,
She, blooming with the bloom of maidenhood.
Nearer and nearer came the angelic band,
And took its station on a rosy cloud
Poised overhead, and from whose wreathéd curves
And shell-like involutions, lightning played
Innocuous, in sportive, flashing forks—
Itself a spectacle of rarest beauty.
There paused they like a flock of pigeons wild,
When, with accordant wing, they light on trees,
Thus resting in their passage on from land
To land, close nestling in the boughs aloft;
Alow, for food or sport, in autumn, when
The woods are painted in their dolphin hues
To sate our eyes with beauty.
                           From their number,
Two came floating down in graceful flight,
With many a playful curve and airy wheel,
As if on some sweet mission kindly bent,
And having three times circled round the Pair,
And having three times bowed the knee before
The Infant Savior, then, with songs and chants
(Which those upon the clouds accompanied
With music instrumental), they held up
Baskets brimful of most delicious fruit,
Festooned with flowers; smiling, they waved them round,
And thus presented them with rhythmic words:

SONG OF THE ANGELS.

I.

Hail, Mary, hail!
Thou hast had slumber sweet,
　Beautiful heaven-dreams,
　Shelter from mountain streams,
Shelter from tempest's beat.
　Hail, Virgin, hail!

II.

Whilst thou wert sleeping here,
We, from the Central Sun
　Traveled to Lebanon,
Sweet-smelling, snowy-topped,
　Cedar-clad Lebanon.
　Hail, Mother, hail!

III.

Cooled by the mountain's breath,
　There we found ice and snow;
Thence down to Nazareth
　Swiftly we two did go;
Juicy fruits there we found
　On branches high and low,
Pomegranates, apples round,
Citrons, grapes, oranges,
　Sunny-ripe, to and fro
　Waving in winds that blow
　Over the Holy Land.
Take them—both fruit and snow.
　Here is a basketful;
Reach out thy holy hand,
　　Lady!
Reach out thy hand.

IV.

Hark to a silver bell,
High up in heaven's dome,
Sounding so far and soft,
That never mortal ear
Yet heard its ringing clear,
        Save thine,
        Virgin Divine,
        Save only thine,
            Thine;
Fare thee well—fare thee well—
We must aloft.

Then to their compeers stationed on the cloud
The Angel pair ascended cheerily.
Straightway the travelers examined well
The palatable food uppiled within
The woven osier baskets.   Their sweet rhymes
Had spoken truth for once; for poesy,
When genuine, seldom utters what is false.
They found fine wheaten bread, and a small flask
Of wine of Palestine—wine of the best,
Sweet to the smell and sweeter to the taste.
Of this last Blessed Mary gently sipped,
As doth a delicate bird quenching its thirst
Beside a limpid rill.   So, first they made
Their savory supper off the bread and wine,
Both from their birthplace, and both smelt of home,
Both gladdened their pure hearts.   Then, for dessert,
In moderation, but with relish keen,
They ate of those delectable fruits, inwreathed
In flowery garlands, tastefully combined;
And as they did so, oft they called to mind
The hills on which they ripened.   Smell, and taste,

And memory, all were gratified at once,
Both mind and body—heavenly feast indeed!
  Anon their glance they turn to the westering sun,
Which hung bright hovering o'er the mountain-tops,
Soon doomed to sink behind them. Then (sweet sight)
The Infant Savior raised his little hand
And, rosily smiling, pointed to the orb
About to disappear, then turned it east,
Where broken fragments of the rainbow's arch
Were melting soft away.
                    But hark! afar
To westward—faint to mortal ear—but loud
To listening Angel's; hark! the peal
Of silver trumpet coming swiftly on,
And sounding as it came a signal-note,
Which told the advent of another band
Of Angel messengers. From out the cloud
(I mean the cloud of which 't was said before
That lightning played around it), quick there came
An answering trumpet-note, which nearer pealed,
And therefore louder. Quavers two it had,
Between which was a middle note of strength,
The latter quaver tremulous and prolonged,
The first more quick and frequent. Far around
The note resounded,
    " Ta—ta—ta—tan—tan—ra—ra,"
Through echoing caverns, and down gorges deep,
Till all the region round with clangor sweet
Seemed circle-wise o'erflowing.
                    Nearer and nearer,
From strange, far countries not then known to be,
By those in Europe or in Asia born,
They came thus heralded by silver tromp;
They came across the ocean of the west—

'The broad Atlantic—not then crossed by men.
'Mong many curious things, they brought a flower,
A mystic flower, which seemed to symbolize
Some great event, which, in the coming time,
Should mold the world anew.
                  Arrived at length,
They greeted those upon the floating cloud,
As angels greet each other when they meet;
Then one approached, saluted thrice the Pair,
Bowed three times to the Savior of the world
And then, with earnest, kindly air, like one
Who does a painful duty gracefully,
But still against his will, he held the flower
Before her view, reciting all the while
Some verses, very sweet but somewhat sad,
And full of most heart-thrilling mystery,
Which hung, like drapery, around the theme,
Neither concealing it in full from view,
Nor quite revealing it. All this was done
In kindness and with good intent, to pave
The way for coming woes, and blunt their edge.
   The Holy Lady, trembling, reached her hand
And took the flower, half-smiling, weeping half.
She seemed like one who strives to hide her gloom
From those around, lest it might grieve *them* too.
It would not do—the tear ran oozing forth
Adown her virgin cheek, grown suddenly pale.
A shudder o'er her blooming members came,
An instant's shrinking, as when summer sky
Is suddenly overcast, and a wailing wind
Sweeps over some soft, shrinking, sensitive plant.
She knew not what the mystic flower meant,
She could not have expressed her thought in words,
But a strange forefeel of some future woe

Thrilled through her frame, and thus suffused her eyes.
The angel, seeing this, on bended knee,
With wings close-folded, and with bowed-down head,
Remained in pensive posture, wrapped in thought.
Joseph, who, less than she, had understood
What meant the mystic plant, endeavored much
To overcome the force of sympathy;
But all in vain—in vain—
The big tears trickled down his ruddy cheek
And manly beard, like raindrops from wet caves.
  Then stretched the Holy Child his little hands,
As if he wished to grasp the mystic flower,
To scan it, fondle it, mayhap to play with it.
He knew not what it meant still less than they.
The crown of thorns, the spear. the five red wounds,
The triple nails, the scourge, the holy wood,
All the twelve mystic instruments of woe
And glory, all in floral portraiture
Displayed, were there; he knew not what they meant;
And, often laughing through his tears, which came
He knew not why, he strove, with innocent wiles,
To soothe his mother and his foster-sire.
Then the sweet Mother wiped her dropping eyes,
And by a strong exertion calmed her face,
And wrapping carefully the flower up,
As one folds up a sorrow that *may* come
And lays it out of sight, she placed it in
The embroidered pouch that hung beside her belt,
And looked around as if in search of aught
That might divert her thoughts: such object came.
  The kneeling Angel rose, and from his zone
Loosened a gaudy-looking bag, beplumed,
And all with curious shells and beads o'erwrought,
And broideries, such as tropic tribes delight in,

And drew therefrom a sprig of evergreen,
Which he presented thus with dancing rhymes:

> Here are leaves evergreen,
> Close-plaited, thick and dense,
> Not shaking easily,
> Ne'er moving breezily,
> Sweeter than frankincense.
> The tree those leaves grow upon,
> Is not a mighty one,
> Like trees of Lebanon.
> 'Tis not lofty, 'tis not mighty,
> Seems not so to mortal eye;
> Some do call it Arbor Vitæ,
> Ever pointing to the sky.
>
> Steadily, steadily,
> Blow the winds rough or soft,
> It looks to God aloft,
> Like a saint's daily life,
> Green under winter's snow.
> Take these leaves, crush them up,
> They will the sweeter grow,
> Readily, readily,
> Giving their fragrance forth.
> Take these leaves of Arbor Vitæ,
> Crush them, smell them, Lady, try;
> 'Tis not lofty, seems not mighty,
> But points ever to the sky.

The Virgin did as she was bid, and smiled;
The sympathetic smile went round the group.
The Wingéd One then told in simple words
About the evergreen tree, what kind of roots,
Its spread beneath the soil, how it was found
On both the Atlantic shores, but of a kind

Diverse in each.   Then told he of strange birds,
And pointing to the feathered pouch he bore,
He bade her note the plumes so bright, so sheen,
So curious in texture; telling her
How it had once belonged to a savage queen,
Who lived in a green island far across
The ocean wave.   "But promise," first he said,
"To keep what now I tell you a profound
And all-unwhispered secret."   Joseph bowed
And pointed to his lips, and Mary bowed,
And then the Wingéd One narrated thus:
   "The time has not arrived by centuries
Fourteen, when that far distant land, so rich
And grand, shall be made known to those that dwell
On this side the great ocean.   Then shall rise
A pious, subtle-thoughted man o' the sea,
Who, praying much, and studying much, shall sail,
After his hair grows white, across the wave
And reach a wonderful country—a New World.
His very name, as called by his compeers,
Shall seem prophetic of the mighty deed,
So strangely oft are wond'rous world-events
Link'd in a golden chain, with ring in ring,
All closely interwoven and compact.
Christophoro Colombo, his two names!
The first is founded on a future myth
(For many strange myths shall spring up and take
Firm root in the belief of coming men),
Of a vast giant, who shall bear, they'll say,
A Holy Child upon his shoulders broad,
And with him on his back, shall wade across
A deep, wide water (so shall run the legend);
The second name means—or will mean—a dove.
On these two emblems long might fancy brood,

And build a world of wonders. But enough.
Farewell. Receive this trifle. It contains
Some rarities of transatlantic birth,
Which may both please the eye and pique the mind."
   With heartfelt thanks the Virgin took the scrip
Thus wafted to her from an unknown world,
Eying its curious bead and feather work,
Its many-colored plumes and inwrought shells,
Which piqued her fancy to perpetual play,
And caused her think what a sweet task 't would be,
Some future day, when travel-toils were over,
And she snug seated 'midst her early friends,
To scan its new-world treasures. But she vowed
She'd keep the secret closely, firmly locked
Within her inmost heart—she would indeed—
O, what rich realms of wonder and of mirth!
What arch evasive answers, innocent fun!
   These thoughts flashed swiftly through her youthful
      mind
Like gold carp through a pool. But lo! a sight!
A lovely spectacle! The Angel bands,
The *three*, each separate first, and each arrived
From different quoins o' the world, now all combine
In *one*, and with a trinal symphony
Lark-like ascend, all singing as they soar,
Still singing e'en when lost to mortal sight,
The music sweeter as more far it grew,
Upmounting, swelling, opening, spreading out;
To those who stood enthralled below they seemed
The birds of passage of the universe,
Winging their way through heaven from star to star,
And hastening onward to the Central Sun.
   "Now that the sun has set and angels gone,"
Said Joseph firmly, like a man who girds

Himself for a strong effort, "we perforce
Must travel onwards. Night is coming on,
And darkness. We must leave this lonely mount,
This Cave of the Seven Cedars. Who can tell
But that some friendly shepherds may be found
Around the mountain's foot, whose sheltering tents
To-night shall give us hospitable welcome,
And a snug, quiet place wherein to sleep."
　　So saying, their preparations soon were made,
And off they started down the mountain's side.

CANTO VI.

THE BRIDGES.

AS when a thoughtful man of modern days,
　　Wandering through devious wood-roads, o'er the hills,
Oft pauses on some bosky ridge, to list
The voice of torrent floods that roar beside
A railroad's track below, if suddenly
A train of cars comes sliding down the curves,
Now this side, and now that, of the stream's brink,
Whilst these are passing, hears the stream no more,
But gathers all his powers to catch the din,
Now coming, now receding, of the cars,
Soon as the wheels have thundered past, again
Can hear the voice of waters and of pines;
So fared it with our travelers. First, came floods,
With thunder rolling on from cloud to cloud;
Then the rich harmony of angel bands;
But when these all had ceased, they heard from far
And near the floods again, with all the sounds
On nature's steps attendant. Joseph, then,

Thus spake to his companion: "Mother sweet,
Hark how the maddened waters roar, and vex
The air with wildest clamor. Night is coming.
I fear we can not pass the swollen floods
Which, all unbridged, fierce tumble down the hills;
And yet a secret voice within me cries:
'Go on—go on—if water's power is strong,
The power of faith is stronger—man, go on.'
What think'st thou of that voice?"

                              "Obey its hest,"
Said Mary, looking, trustful, up to heaven,
And folding Jesus closer to her breast.
"Obey its hest; thy guardian angel speaks,
Unseen, but hovering near. Since we have been
Upon this journey, firmly I believe
We never, night or day, have been alone;
And whilst our thoughts keep pure, our aims sincere,
Alone we ne'er shall be. Bad spirits loosed from hell,
And evil demons ranging round the world,
May still be on the watch to do us hurt,
And harm this Holy Being in my arms;
But vain shall be their efforts whilst we two
Are faithful to ourselves and true to Him;
Therefore, lead forward."

                              Forwards still they went.
It was an antique mountain road, deep-worn
By years of travel; sumpter-mules in lines,
Mule after mule, slow-stepping up the rocks
Or down them, often passed these perilous heights,
The drivers cheering them with songs the while,
As still is done in Spain; and had the storm
Not swelled the streams, or swept away each bridge,
It still were passable to man or beast.
But scarcely had they traveled half a league,

Before a turbid watercourse, loud-voiced
And swift and turbulent, rushed athwart their way,
Seeming to bar all passage.   Stock still stood
The beast which Joseph led, aghast with fear;
Far-darkening shadows fell from rocks around,
Making the dusk of evening still more dread.
" A gloomy spot to spend the night."   " Indeed,
'Twould be so—but more gloomy still to turn
And to retrace our steps which we have ta'en
With mickle toil adown the the channeled rocks,
And gloomier still than all the thought that we
Were traveling evèn half a league towards the spot
Where dwells the blood-stained tyrant we are flying."
    Behold! thought-quick a stable, one-arched bridge,
Reared without human hands, with lighted lamps
On either side, uprose and spanned the flood,
As if inviting them to pass.   Without
One shudder of alarm, one tremor slight,
They passed the bridge, by faith led on, by faith
Upheld.   Scarce had they cleared its two-fold grades,
Before, with sudden crash, the mass gave way,
And down were swept its timbers and its piers,
And, whirling round and round, were quickly dashed
Sheer o'er the toppling precipice that yawned
On one side of the bridge; the waterfall
Swift sucked them down, and in an instant's time
The structure all had vanished.
                              " Fearful sight,"
Said Mary, clasping firmer her sweet charge,
And looking up to heaven with thankful heart.
"Greater the peril, sweeter the escape,"
Said Joseph, moving briskly down the mount,
With firm hand leading forward the awed beast
So that he might not stumble.   " In our dreams

This may come back to us, perhaps; and, waking,
How sweet to feel that danger there is none,
And that the bridge, with all its planks and lights,
Shall fall no more for us; even to see
It falling, after we have passed its arch,
Makes all the blood run cold." They traveled on.
    Downwards in savage zigzags, ever down,
The solitary track conducted them
Past many a scene of horror; under crags
Which, toppling overhead, threatened to fall
If loosened by a breath; by dizzy brinks,
One glance at which inflicted thoughts of·terror
Blacker than dreams of nightmare. More than once
Some vast o'erhanging rock far off was heard,
. Torn from its base by hungry, eating floods,
To tumble headlong down with all its pines,
Dread echoing round the mountains. Quite as wild,
But not so startling to them was it once,
When, from an open roadside space, they caught
A glimpse of the new moon, about to sink
Behind the topmost peak of the whole range;
One of her sharp horns even then was hid,
As though behind that wild, chaotic pass
She meant to plunge to nothing. Such fine scenes,
So dear to painter's or to poet's eye,
Are not without their use in this hard world,
And ofttimes drive the thoughts from centering self
In ever-widening circles round the world,
Or, nobler still, conduct them up to God.
Thus was it with that pious-hearted pair,
Slow traveling down the mountain's darkening side.
The sense of danger had not so benumbed
Their loftier feelings that they could not gaze
With rapture on such spectacles. Thank God,

They thought of God, whilst gazing on the moon.
    Still, ever downward!   Joseph said, at last:
"I think I hear beneath us a full stream
Which, having overflowed its natural banks,
Has widened so its bounds, that we, perforce,
Must rest all night beside its rushing flood."
"I hear its mighty voice, too," Mary said,
Although no tremor mingled with her speech
To mar its silvery sweetness; "but I think
That we shall pass its waves, however wide,
And travel o'er its flood, however deep,
And reach the other shore, however far;
And that nor flood nor fire shall stop our course,
Until we gain the shepherds' sheltering tents."
    Ere long they reached an open, treeless knoll,
From 'which they viewed the prospect stretching dim
Beneath the starlight, and beheld a stream
Which, broad and long and rapid in its flow,
Rolled on in dusky grandeur through the night,
With such a deep-toned, melancholy roar
As made the very stars in heaven look sad.
As thus they stood at gaze, and vainly strove,
By aid of the far stars (too vastly far
To illumine objects on this nether earth),
Behold! again that wonderful Light 'gan beam
From the Almighty Child, which now and then
(Not always) issued in mysterious streams—
Light which the angels could not understand—
An effluence differing from known solar light
In many ways—though softer, more intense;
More luminous, but less dazzling; though serene,
All-perceant; though as bland as olive oil,
As penetrative as the electric spark;
Diffusive, mystic, increate, unknown.

As mariners watch the changes of the tide,
The Virgin Mother, with attentive eye,
Since the Child's birth had watched its ebbs and flows;
But still she understood it not—knew not
Whence or how came it, or by what strange laws
Its intermitted efflux was evolved;
But oft, deep musing, in her secret heart
She thought that as it seldom or ever shone
Except when the God-Child was sunk in sleep,
That visions of his ante-natal life
Perhaps were then bright-flashing through his brain
Like summer lightnings through a sleeping cloud
At sunset, when the air is all serene,
And earth wrapt up in dreams. At such times, too,
Soft-wreathing smiles were often seen to pass
Across his infant features beautiful,   .
Like silvery iceblinks seen in polar seas
When Northern Lights are dancing, and starred Night
Seems lovelier than proud Day.
                                    Then they beheld
Distinct that storm-fed river. What before
Seemed a wild waste of waters dim and dark,
Now gleamed with silvery splendor. They could tell
The natural bed of the stream, when at its full,
From the broad border of wave-covered marsh
On either side, bedecked with washy ooze.
Beyond it a rich tract of table-land
Stretched southward in far upward-rising slope,
Where lovely clumps of trees were intermixed
With pastures; and still further (wished-for sight),
Sweet shepherd tents all gleaming in the glow
Of that clear primal light. With joy they eyed
First the lit landscape, then the sleeping Babe,
Then one another's faces, heaven-illumed.

As when, in early pioneering days,
Some hunter or bold trapper of the west,
Roaming beneath the Rocky Mountain range,
Would start ere dawn of day, while yet the stars
Were shining, and should reach a bluff
From whose tall top he views an unknown stream
Rolling in dusky gloom—Nebraska's wave,
Or Niobrara green with groves of pine—
Musing and gazing much he falls asleep—
He sleeps—he wakes—the scene before so weird
Now brightens, for, behold! the sun is up,
And up he takes his gun, and hies in quest
Of game, and shouts for joy, and leaps adown
The bluff: such to these two appeared the change,
When that Divine Effulgence, raying forth,
Opened the rich, wide prospect.
                    Then again,
Singing, they journeyed down the mountain's side
Towards the water's brink, as pilgrim bands
In after-days were wont their souls to cheer
When onwards to Loretto's shrine they paced,
Hallowing the way with music.
                    At the stream
Arrived, they pause in silence for a time
To list its rueful voice, with hearts deep hushed,
And some slight touch of terror.   Then the Child
Waking from slumber, lo! the splendor fades,
And double darkness, streaming fog-like up,
Close-wrapt them sudden round like a black pall,
Made drearier by contrast.   Quite as long,
As one might count a score in measured speech,
They tarried in the darkness by the flood's
Wave-tortured shore, absorbed in anxious thought,
And almost frenzied by the boisterous swirl

Of breaking, dashing billows—
When, lo, a light!—a thousand lights at once
Flash in long-streaming lines across a bridge!
   A bridge upreared in darkness! but complete
In all its parts, pier, buttress, balustrade,
Arch after arch of lordly span, from shore
To shore conducting, by a lustrous path
Above the waters, to the other side.
Nor wanted holy harpers stationed round
On airy minarets from point to point
Along the lighted pathway—sweet their hymns,
And sweet the golden instruments they played.
And loftier still, in center of the bridge
A many-colored campanile rose,
With marvelous chimes of bells by angels rung
In answer to the harpers lower down.
And sometimes bells and harps paused for a time,
A little interval, when cymbals loud
Resounding struck the waters, struck the sky,
And made the firm bridge tremble.   Prelude this
To a much softer music, which arose
Softer and sweeter from a smaller set
Of delicatest bells, fine-toned, fine-tuned,
Of silver some, and some of purest gold,
More dulcet than the bells of Fairyland;
And rhythmic flutes, and musical glasses played
By seraph-fingers round the moistened brim;
And, what was charming more than all the rest,
Than flutes or glasses or harmonicons,
Angelic voices in rich unison
Saluted, as he passed, the Son of God,
The Virgin pure saluted.   O, 'twas sweet
And jubilant, that passage o'er the bridge!
   Entranced, they scarce had reached the other shore,

11

When all the wonder-structure 'gan dissolve.
Quenched were the lights, the harpers flew to heaven,
The singers, ringers, flutists, disappeared;
By some strange spell the solid wood and stone
Seemed gradual changed to water. From above
Downwards the magic transformation ran,
Melting the fabric; campanile first,
Then minaret, then balustrade and floor,
Buttress and pier, one after one became
A fluid mass, and streaming graceful down,
And mingling gently with the torrent flood,
All vanished!' Twas too beautiful to last.
   One only bridge does history tell us of
Which bore some semblance to that heavenly one;
So faintly can the sons of earth approach,
By studied effort and prefixed design,
To what the angels do as if in sport.
'Twas at that joyous season when all Greece,
All Asia Minor, and the neighbor isles
Were wont in pilgrim-bands to throng to Delos,
When, in a single night, the narrow strait,
Which parts Rhenea from Apollo's isle,
Was overspanned, as if by magic art,
With a most gorgeous structure. Up it rose
In darkness and the silence of the night
(The parts having all beforehand been prepared
In Athens, and thence secretly conveyed),
And lo! when morning dawned it stood complete,
Arch after arch bedecked with thousand flags
And blazoned banners waving. Jocund bands
Of rosy virgins, bands of blooming youth,
Chanting sweet pæans 'neath the rising sun,
Whom thronging nations gazed on with delight,
Across its airy arches danced along,

Bearing rich gifts to Phœbus. 'Twas indeed
A gala-bridge, delicious to the sight,
And ne'er to be forgotten.
    But to return. The far side of the flood,
Or that to which the Holy Family passed,
Had all along its length a wall of cloud,
Which stood unmoved until the bridge dissolved.
'Twas broad below and pillarwise above,
And rose to highest heaven—
Like that which led the Israelites of old
Across the desert sands. Its hither side
Shekinah-bright appeared, the other dark,
And fashioned so that neither eye nor ear
Could penetrate its substance. As they moved
Along their journey, soft to right and left
It opened like a folding door of haze, .
And gave the travelers exit, melting soon
Both with its light and darkness into air.
Behind them rolled the river wild and dark,
But ever more and more they left the gloom,
And 'gan ascend that upward-sloping tract
Which gently led them on to higher grounds   •
And more alluring prospects. Meteors bright
With brilliant trails of splendor streaming from
The zenith southwards seemed to beckon them on;
Incessant play of sheen electric gleams
(Signs, mayhap, of a far-receding storm)
Flashed round the horizon, bringing to quick view
Clouds of fantastic shape, and clumps of trees,
And pastoral flocks and herds and distant tents.
These objects came to sight or disappeared
In rapid sequence, as the strange light lived
Or died. Such sudden gleams of prospect are
Often the most attractive; silvery-soft

They open to the view delightful scenes,
Then close them—fancy does the rest—the eye
Is pleased, not sated—and the spell-bound soul,
Forever looking forth for something new,
Enjoys the *seen*, and pictures forth with joy
More lovely things *unseen* and yet to come.

CANTO VII.

THE ARAB ENCAMPMENT.

SOMETIMES they passed a little, slumb'rous grove
Of fair acacia trees, with delicate leaves
Close-folded in deep sleep; anon a breeze,
Suddenly whispering, strewed the fragrant air
With showers of snow-white blossoms; then a gush
Of music from some dulcet nightingales,
Nestling unseen among the thorny boughs,
Charmed trees and listening stars; and ever still
New streams of perfume floated o'er their path,
And·sweeter flowers opened on the night,
And others sweeter still. Like stars of earth,
Among the foliage and above the trees,
Sparkled unnumbered fire-flies.
                              On they passed
In silence mostly, for such pleasing thoughts
Becalmed them both, that neither wished to speak.
At last the Virgin Mother, in these words,
Commenced to think aloud: "Since Gabriel came
And in my lowly home at Nazareth
Announced to me the coming wonder-birth,
This earth has scarce seemed earth. I know not how,
Sometimes it seems to me as though I lived

Wrapt round and round in some high, holy dream,
Like a bright rosy cloud with a spirit in it,
While other clouds, far off, some not so bright,
And some with thunderbolts but half concealed,
Send forth low, muttering peals.   Things once so strange
Seem strange no longer—wonder seems *no* wonder;
That glorious gala-bridge o'er which we passed,
Uprose not unexpected in the dark,
And all its magic music, fresh from heaven,
Seemed scarce more high-entrancing than the trills
Of those small nightingales which now we hear
Sweet-quavering 'midst acacias.   This fresh path,
Bordered with flowers, which, gently winding, leads
O'er upland pastures and past blossoming trees,
Could scarce be sweeter did it lead to heaven;
And those balsamic odors of the night,
Forever varying as we move along,
Seem not one whit inferior to the breath
Of golden censers fuming, angel-swung.
Yes, from the time that Gabriel spoke to me
And told me of the things which were to come,
The commonest things of earth have hallowed been—
My lowly village home appeared transformed,
The same and not the same.   The village girls,
With whom I oft had sported, gathered round,
And led me to the fields in search of flowers,
And to the woods, to peep into the nests,
And to the emerald meadows, there to dance,
And to the village fountain, vase in hand,
And to the hills at night, to watch the stars;
But everywhere, in town, or field, or woods,
Methought I stood in heaven; and as the lark
May be supposed, whilst in her lowly nest
Among the clods, to dream of dayspring clear,

And of glad caroling among the clouds,
And of rich cantos sung above the earth,
So did I dream, both day and starry night,
Of splendors high-celestial. Then I went
To see my cousin in the hill-country,
Whom, when I had saluted, straight she felt
The babe leap in her womb for very joy,
And prophesied of glorious things to come,
Calling me ' Mother of her Lord.' Then more
Than ever earth seemed heaven to me—although
Scarce more than now it does. But see those herds
Of cattle to our left—how numerous!
And to our right, far on the highest hills,
What endless flocks of sheep! and, further on,
Camels and kids and asses! Lo! it seems
As though some patriarch of the olden time,
With all his flocks and herds and clustered tents,
Had settled down upon this grassy slope
For pasture."
      Joseph raised his eyes, and looked
Around with scrutinizing glance, and scanned
The pastoral landscape. "Need of caution now.
Perhaps some nomad chief or Arab sheik,
Near us encamped, may be among those tents."
Mary let down her vail. "Be cautious, dearest.
Conceal from view the few things we may have
Of any value." Mary from her ears
Unloosed her pendants formed of opal stone,
Eight-rayed, and set in purest gold. "Be sure
Thou dost not let them see the golden cup
One of the wise men gave us." She replied:
"The cup is safely stowed away within
The sackcloth bag upon the donkey's back,
And no one e'er will dream of things so rich

In such poor wrappings." Joseph stroked his beard,
And spoke like one communing with himself:
"Well—very well—the cup is safe, I think,
The gold, the jewels, and the precious myrrh,
The earrings and the bracelets and gold chains—
All safe within the sack—so far, so good—
My prized papyrus scroll is in my pouch,
And if it were not, no one here could read it;
All safe, I think, all well concealed from view,
All safe. But we perhaps must needs confront
The owner of these herds. I hope he may
Not prove a ruffian and remove thy veil—
Such outlaws may be found—and, Virgin Mother,
The feather-fringed scrip the angel gave thee?"
Mary unloosed it from the broidered belt,
And placed it in the sack; the belt itself
She also thus arranged, and a rough cord
She tied around her waist, and all was fixed.

A furlong thence they reached some circling tents,
High overtopped by many a lofty palm.
Addressing some they saw reposing there
On the green turf, the men began to stare
As though they understood not; but at last,
By signs and words Semitic (they were Arabs),
Joseph made them conceive the thing he meant.
Then did they lead the travelers slowly on
To where the chieftain sat within his tent,
Upon a gorgeous cushion stretched at ease,
Playing some game of chance with one who seemed
His favorite wife (another tent hard by
Contained some other wives and concubines);
And Joseph told his story then so well
(The chief knew well the tongue of the holy land),
And answered all his questions with such skill,

Divulging just enough to satisfy
But not betray, and all with so much grace,
Such show of openness and want of guile,
That the pleased chief, half robber though he was,
Gave orders that the travelers should be served
With the best fare his tented home could yield.
And, better to insure this end, he told
Some trusty servitors, with utmost care,
To lead the Lady to his mother's tent,
And give her to that matron's kindly charge
Till morrow morn—for Joseph had made known
His wish to start ere daybreak. All went well.

 Joseph himself was shown a vacant tent,
Where all his wants were cared for, and his beast's.
On leaving then the sheik, he viewed again,
What he had merely glanced at as he went,
The beautiful Arab mares (five hundred told)
Tethered at proper intervals around
The lodging of their lord. Beside the mares
Stood sentinels, all armed in Arab guise,
To watch one quarter of the night, and then
To be relieved by fresh ones. Lamps hung round
Suspended to the palms, or raised on poles,
And piles of arms were stacked in warlike pomp,
Ready for instant use.
   The Virgin Mother
Was by that antique Arab dame received
With show of utmost kindness. Long she gazed
Upon her youthful beauty; longer still
Upon the Godlike beauty of the Child.
Such holy, heavenly eyes! She ne'er had seen
Aught like them. Then, those graceful, curling locks!
Through which such gleams of light seemed intertwined,
That much as she admired them, a strange awe

Stole over her.   Never had she seen such light
Round any human head.   It seemed at times
As though around his curls a thin, thin circlet
Of delicatest texture came and went,
Now melting into nothing, now aglow,
Like rainbows round a mist-hung waterfall,
And still she gazed and gazed, until her eyes,
Which often had absorbed the desert's glare,
Shone like an ancient Sibyl's.   Lo! her lips
'Gan move with fitful motion—much she spoke
In rhythmic measure in the Arab tongue,
Which Blessed Mary understood not fully,
Although she thought it seemed like prophecy.
At last that ancient mother fell asleep,
The Infant sweetly slumbered, and the Virgin,
After her wanderings long, sank to repose,
And all within the tent were hushed to rest.

BOOK III.

BORDERLAND—Continued.

CANTO I.

MYSTERY OF SOUND—MYSTERY OF WATER.

SO deep had been the Virgin's sleep that night,
So sweet, so pure, so hushed, so holy calm,
Almost it seemed like sleep of saintly death.
Thus soul and body, which had been outworn
By the long travel of the day before,
Were perfectly restored to wonted strength,
And not before two hours ere dawn of day
Did any cloudlike dream float o'er the blue
Of slumber.   Then a vision beautiful
Entered her brain; then Gabriel she saw
In garb and feature such as when he came
To announce the advent of the Savior Lord,
And thus unto her ear he softly spoke:
 " Mary, arise! the morning star is up;
Another day of journeying must begin.
Arise, and for the pilgrimage prepare.
I will awaken Joseph, who will be
In fitting time before the tent-door, ready
With all required needments.   Fresh and cool
Is breath of coming dawn."

Then Mary rose,
And the old Arab mother also rose,
Subservient to the wishes of her guest.
Her maids she also roused, and bade them fetch
Pure water from the spring, and napkins clean,
Ewer and basin, all that was required
For that more common and recurrent rite
Of daily baptism, type of one more high
And spiritual.   In an inner space,
Veiled and partitioned from the common room,
The Virgin and the Child remained enshrined
As long as needful was; then fresh and bright,
As morning star uprising from the sea,
Effulgent she came forth, and filled the tent
With splendor.   Then again that antique dame,
In reverent posture bending to the earth,
Worshiped the Holy Child, and all her maids,
With an instinctive reverence, worshiped too,
Much wondering why their knees were drawn to earth,
And whence that more than starry radiance came.
   " Ho!"—Joseph's voice from outside cheerful rang—
"All hail, beloved of heaven, come forth, come forth;
The morning star is singing blithe for joy,
Although we hear him not; all dewy-fresh,
Cool Night still wears some jewels in her crown,
Ere long compelled to lay them gradual by,
Until her coronation-time returns.
Come forth! an angel orders, quick, come forth."
   Blessing and blessed, the Virgin issued forth,
As yet unveiled, beneath the holy stars,
And as the doubled splendor moved along,
The Infant Savior gazed upon the sky
With his sweet, lustrous eyes, and waved his hands,
And jumped in his mother's arms, and crowed and laughed.

And crowed again, as though he meant to say
To those far worlds, "Good morning." On they went,
Silent at first, for near a fragrant mile,
With gaze still upward turned, as though the earth,
Fresh as it was and dewy, had for them
But slight attraction when compared with heaven;
A three-fold silent worship! From afar
The voice of floods and water-courses roared,
Telling full ruefully of recent storms,
And sounding like the din of dying war;
And as the travelers slowly journeyed on,
Old earth appeared to thrill through all her bulk
As though some mystic Power were passing then,
Oracular, dim-booming. Lamp on lamp
The lights were waxing faint in heaven's high vault,
And that dusk point of time came creeping on,
When, for brief season, heaven seems growing gray,
And earth, being not yet lighted, the vast world
Seems brown with lingering twilight.
                              Then arose
Two voices, bass and treble, sweetly tuned,
Singing a psalm of David; whilst a third,
A tenor, thrilling on through boundless space,
Through earth, through air, through all the fading stars,
Accompanied the human chant, and rose
Or fell, swelled up, or died away, or paused,
As it did, forming one accordant mass
Of harmony, the music of all worlds,
A mighty diapason formed of all,
All-interpiercing, all-embracing, grand.
    Before the psalm was finished, all the stars
Had faded; Phosphor vanishing last. As when
In some magnificent cathedral, all
The services being ended, silent crowds

Pace, thoughtful, down the aisles towards the door,
The solemn organ pealing all the while,
Until the worshipers have disappeared,
So, whilst that chant was sounding, star on star,
Evanishing with slow and solemn tread,
Left heaven's broad aisles—and Night, close-muffled, shut
Her mighty minster-doors.
                         Soon daybreak came,
Whose delicate, rosy hues scarce tinged the east,
Before they 'gan to fade, all flooded o'er
And swallowed up in sunshine.   Then was heard
The song of skylark mounting up to heaven;
Then every nested tree sent forth a stream
Of melody composed of various notes,
And such a piping, trilling, warbling rose,
All intermixed, all in confusion heaped,
That had the notes been louder, or less sweet,
The discord would have jarred upon the ear.
  "Each sings as best he can," said Joseph, whilst
They passed a grove of trees where such a choir
Of birds was chanting—"each as best he can.
Perhaps there may be men with ears so fine,
With such a full and perfect grasp of sound,
With such a knowledge of the song of birds,
That when they, hear so many, all at once,
They can take in the whole, and every part,
And each melodious gush, each tiny rill
Of music, flowing many ways at once,
May be collected, grasped, retained, and held
Until the brain takes cognizance of all.
Such men there well may be, and such I think
There are.   Hence, 'tis not past belief, that when
On Sabbath days, through all the Holyland,
In temple, synagogue, and private room,

A million voices rise at once in prayer,
Or hymns of thanksgiving, the Ear Supreme
Can clasp them all, no still, small voice unheard,
No faintest note unheeded."
       " Even so,"
Said Mary, pointing to a blasted tree;
" As at a single glance the rolling eye
Takes in trunk, branches, bough, and spray
Of yon tall oak, with all its intricate
Complexity of network, shoot, and twig,
So does the Ear of God, as I believe,
Catch every rustle of the smallest leaf
That shakes on every tree round all the earth,
The sound of every wave on every shore,
The note of every bird in every land,
The faintest voice of every blade of grass,
Or tiniest buzz of smallest insect's wing."
  Then Joseph answered thus, in thoughtful mood:
" The brain turns giddy when we strive to grasp
The mysteries of Godhead; when we brood
In fancy o'er the congregated sounds
Of all creation,
From thunderclaps and dashing cataracts
Down to the chirp of cricket in the grass,
The loud, the soft, the musical, the harsh,
The myriad sighs and pants and sobs and shouts,
Death-groans and merriest laughter, all combined,
And each distinctly heard."
       Thus they, in thought,
On fancy's ladder strove to mount to God,
Like two brave-hearted climbers on the Alps,
Rising from height to height, forever still
Straining to catch some glimpse of the Supreme.
At last they reach the highest—and look forth

In hopes to see Him, and behold Him not—
But by the effort braced and prospect cheered,
And having scanned more of His works the while,
A mightier God he seems than aye before,
A mightier and a nearer; so, to these,   ·
The matin song of birds, the earliest heard,
Led them from thought to thought successive up,
Until thought's instrument, the laboring brain,
Grown dizzy, told them they had seen enough,
And bade them thence descend.
                      Ere long they left
Those grassy slopes and meads, where they had seen
The nomads in their tents, and, winding up
The crowning ridge, came to a region wild
And lone and savage; gorges black as death,
With cedars overbrowed and wailing pine,
Yawned round them and before them; on they moved,
Now passing o'er a tremulous rustic bridge
Which spanned a deep ravine; now creeping on
Along a breakneck mule-path, stony and rough;
Now wading through a brawling mountain brook;
Now hanging on a toppling precipice,
Where one false step were death. The sun new-risen
Was masked from view, or only shot his beams
Athwart the topmost peaks or loftiest pines,
Or now and then, with narrow fringe of light,
Through some side-opening in the riven rocks,
Gleamed through a mass of shadow.
                      "Ho! a land,"
Said Joseph, "where a hunter might rejoice.
Here hart and hind must find a pleasant home.
Up yonder airy cliff the mountain goat
Has often clambered, often slumbered, too,
Fearless of vulture's beak, or sweep of winds,

As sweetly and securely as, last night,
You, loveliest, slumbered in the robber's tent."
    Along the shadowy gorge they journeyed slow,
Observant of the sylvan scene around.
Sly foxes peeped at them and slunk away;
The agile squirrel leaped from tree to tree,
Arching his tail; the coney of the rock
Looked at them as they passed, and slid from view;
Aloft from some tall peak the eagle rose,
Far sailing o'er the loftiest mountain-tops
As though he spurned his eyrie as too low.
Once, from the tallest height which they had reached,
They saw far, far below a river of mist,
Which, rising from a rivulet's narrow bed,
Filled all a hollow vale from side to side,
And showed the windings of the stream that fed it.
All billowy and grand, though made of vapor,
It rolled and spread, and in the distance looked
Like real moving water.
                "Beautiful,"
Said Joseph, pointing to the mimic stream,
"Are most of the many forms which water takes,
Though some are also fearful.   Type of love
And of destruction!   Emblem of the might
And the beneficence of the Supreme,
How various are the shapes thou canst assume,
How awful and how lovely!   Threadlike rills
Thou leadest now adown smooth emerald slopes;
Now, Samson-like, thou shak'st the pillared globe
As if thou strov'st to wrench it from its base,
And whelm the whole in ruin."
                        Here he paused,
And like a singer who, in key too high,
Has tuned his descant, in a lower note
Continued thus.

"Even ice is beautiful,
With pictured surface mimicking the form
Of fern, or feathers, spray, or tapering twigs,
Or pine leaves needle-shaped.
Most beautiful is frost when seen upon
Thin-bladed grass, or candying mossy rocks;
And as for flakes of snow, O! I have watched them
With wonder, on the sides of Lebanon,
When I was there among the woodcutters,
And often did I scan their curious figures
When newly-fallen—stars, and spokéd wheels,
And many lovely shapings crystalline.
All these are forms of water—all are fair—
And see "—he pointed to the other side,
Where, opposite the opening which disclosed
The vaporous river, streamed a waterfall
Of slender body but of dizzy height,
Down-misting, wide out-streaming from the rock
Like the Swiss Staubbach—"see yon cataract
(If so it may be called), how it melts away
To rainbowed mist before it reaches earth—
Can aught in nature be more beautiful?
Then see "—he pointed to the other side—
"That stream of volumed fog that fills yon vale,
Like distant river rolling dreamlike on;
And see "—and now he pointed overhead—
"Those wingéd waters wafted o'er the sky,
Those locked-up lakes afloat through heaven's vault,
Those voyaging reservoirs, from land to land
Sailing; those cisterns sealed, which, when the time
Has come, will pour down on the thirsty.fields
Effusion bland—are they not beautiful?"
  "Indeed they are," said Mary, smiling sweet,
"Most fair are clouds whenever they appear,

12

Except when blackening into thunderstorms;
And so are subterranean streams, if we
Could see them with the eye as they are seen
By fancy, flowing, gurgling up and down
In million-fold meanders, small and large,
Vein linked to vein, a labyrinthine maze.
Most fair is water e'en when forced by art
To rise in jets, and, arching graceful round,
To overflow, and fall in circular sheet
Around a marble basin's rounded rim.
Fair is it, seen from airy bridge's arch,
With gentle current ever gliding on,
Aye coming, going, like a stream of thought;
Fair, when in graceful aqueduct it bears
The mountain's gelid freshness to the town.
Before the earth was born, and all was void,
God's Spirit moved upon the water's face.
It keeps the globe we live on fresh and green;
It bore the Ark above the highest hills;
It started from the rock at Moses' touch;
It purifies, it cleanses; only when
It *stagnates*, does it lose its lustral power,
And turn to poison.   I have said enough."

CANTO II.

HALT BY A WAYSIDE SPRING.

AT noon they reached a ridge of wooded hills
Which, having mounted, on the other side,
Below the brow, beneath a towering rock,
O'ercanopied with ivy and wild vines,
They found a limpid spring.   A place it seemed
Of ancient pilgrimage and rural mirth;

For, all around it, on the emerald sward,
Were circles, such as fairies used to make
Around enchanted fountain and green mead,
When fairies haunted earth. By human feet
Those rings had rounded been; though at the time
The travelers reached them, dancers there were none.
The cool, delicious spot invited them
With voice of lapsing waters, tumbling down
The slope below them, and with whispering leaves,
Till noonday heats were passed, to check their course,
To slake their thirst, and to enjoy repose.
Below them, in the distance, pastoral pipes
Were heard in dreamy cadence sweet and soft,
Steeping the listener most deliciously
In happy visions of the Golden Age,
When shepherds all were blessed, and war and hate
Were names unknown on earth.
How cool that fountain's lymph; how musical
Those seven-reeded, clear Pandean pipes;
How sweet the breath of wildflower-scented breeze;
How soft the feel of turf around that spring;
How cosily, amid the clustering leaves
That draped the rocks, the birds peeped from their nests!
All the five inlets of the human temple,
Like the five portals of a sacred church,
Received, each one, its pious worshipers;
The senses five were sated, and the soul
Sunk in elysian dreams.
                The Holy Child,
With more than wonted glee, began to laugh,
And gambol on the Virgin's youthful lap,
Twisting her ringlets into lovelier curls,
Kissing her rosy dimples—laughing still—
And frolicking with ever-varying wiles,

As joyous children do.   They two, the Child
And the Child's Virgin Mother, sported then,
As oft two angel-children sport in heaven,
When circling seraphs drop their golden harps,
To watch their innocent gambols, and to glad
All heaven with rosier smiles.

      Joseph, meanwhile,
Low-seated on the bench of turf, looked on,
And tears of ecstasy came oozing forth,
And, as they trickled down his ruddy cheek,
He knew not whence they came.   How his big heart,
So pure, so human, throbbed within his breast
With feelings human-heavenly, such as he
Had never felt before or had conceived!
Soon a sweet, wakeful calm crept softly o'er
All three, broke only by a silent gleam
Of happiness, expressed by looks, not words,
As when, o'er twilight heavens some summer eve,
Sweet lightnings play without the smallest sound
Of thunder e'en from far; such was the calm
Which hushed them, sweeter than the calm of sleep.

 Then, wafted on an aromatic breeze,
A butterfly of exquisite beauty came
And lit upon the Child-God's little hand,
And 'gan to ope and shut its winglets four,
As if to show their pictures and their gloss.
It was of that peculiar kind which men
Who study insects, birds, and shells, and flowers,
Have named Apollo; white its silk-soft wings,
White and transparent near the shapely tips—
Cream-white all four, with borders velvet-black—
And on the lower ones two beauty-spots
Eye-shaped, inclosed in carmine-colored rings;
The spots were outlined black, cream-white within—

Type of the spirit-eyes within the soul.
The Infant Savior smiled—the Virgin smiled,
And still the painted wonder oped and closed
Its tiny seraph-pinions.
     Then the Child,
Watching the time when all the wings were raised
Erect above its back, with finger and thumb
Of his right hand (it rested on the left)
Seized it with touch so exquisitely soft,
So Godlike delicate, that not one line
Of beauty was defaced—no, not one hue
Of plumy picturing was erased or smutched—
And ever smiling rosier than at first,
HE raised it in the breeze, and left it free
To circle heavenward. Then HE clapped his hands
Till out of sight it floated, like a boy
Who, on some dewy morning, sees a lark
Soar, jocund, from a meadow to the skies;
Thus flew that Psyche from the Savior's hand
Freed, freshened, beautified, more buoyant grown.

  Then long the Virgin Mother mused and mused,
And still the charming wonder charmed her more,
Till fancy, self-perplexed and riddle-bound,
Dissolved in its own workings.
     Soon, again,
A lovely insect lighted on the Child,
This time, a seven-spotted lady-bird.*
The mother, then, as mothers oft are wont,
Began to count the mystic spots aloud,
Bidding the Child repeat them after her,
Thus giving him, with many a dimpled smile,
His first and ne'er-forgotten lesson in
The holy lore of *numbers.* Soon He could

    * Coccinella septempunctata.

Re-word them without error up to seven,
The holiest of them all, as then was thought.
    The foster-sire, seeing how quickly He
Treasured the numbered spots within his brain,
Remembering every name with perfect ease,
Then rising, took his pilgrim's staff in hand,
And bade the Mother bear the CHILD along
To where a little patch of silvery sand
Had bubbled from the spring, and edged its brim,
Forming a natural tablet, blank and clear—
Then, with his staff's point, marking in the sand
(As ancient sages in their schools were wont
When teaching mathematics), drew distinct
The sacred Hebrew letters, one by one,
From Aleph down to Heth, and spoke aloud
Each letter's name, and bade the Child repeat
Them after him, with voice articulate
As childish lips could speak them—
Then bade him count them—and then added three
Additional letters—Heth, Teth, lastly Jod,
Telling their names and numbers o'er and o'er—
Then held his twice five opened fingers up,
And counted off full ten upon their tips;
And so the Child received the lesson first
In these mysterious signs which are the keys
To unlock the doors of all the sciences,
The sacred elements which spell the Word,
The marks which God himself impressed on stone
With His own finger—writing down His Law.
    The Child seemed much delighted with the task,
And, as he still soft-babbled o'er and o'er
The letters and the figures, holy light
'Gan play around his glossy ringlets bright,
And delicate rainbows (two in number) came

And went, vanished and formed, appeared and dis-
Appeared, their loveliness increasing with
Each change.   One, ever as it came, displayed
The seven listed colors oftenest seen;
The other, like a secondary bow,
More striking in its faintness, showed but three,
Together forming thus the cyclic ten.

Then Joseph, struck with wonder, cried aloud:
"Palmoni," sinking reverent on his knees,
And breaking forth in prayer devout and deep. ·

Behold! along the winding path, which led
Up from the valley, came two shepherd lads,
Curly and blooming, with a damsel fair,
Their still more lovely sister.   In their hands
They bore sweet pipes with seven-graded reeds,
And baskets full of fruit, and bread, and wine,
Intending by that airy hill-top fount
To feast and dance, to sing, and to make merry.

Seeing the Holy Family by the spring,
They were abashed, and turned to run away;
But Mary called them with a voice so sweet,
They needs must turn again—and Joseph called—
And the Child called as loud as call he could
(The louder still the sweeter), and they came.

They came with baskets full, and open hearts,
And shared the bread and wine with those they loved,
Though strangers to them.   O, communion sweet!
Of wine the quantity was fitly scant;
The parents, being good and pious folk,
According to their gifts of time and place
(They lived in caves, and not in nomad tents),
Had meted out such portion of rich wine
(Mellowed by age) as might suffice to give
A kind of consecration to the feast.

What had been portioned out with care for *three*,
Of course was still more scant diffused through *five*,
But still the spirit-symbol was the same—
Blood of the grape—and that of choicest kind—
Old, mellow, purified, and fiery-bland,
Drop-wise effective.   Moderation thus,
Like a veiled priestess, with clean hands, pure heart,
Abuses not the gifts which serve as types
Of richer gifts stored in the spirit-world.

  Thus, having feasted with their new-found friends,
They tuned their seven-stopped pipes and played their best;
And whilst those piped, the sweet, gazelle-eyed girl
Sang a strange, old-world ditty, which, she said,
Had chanted been by damsels ere the Flood.
It was both sad and sweet, both wild and soft,
And often, with its simple touches, drew
Tears down the listener's cheek.
                         And then they danced
A kind of fountain-dance around the spring,
More gracefully than fairies ever danced,
When fairies haunted earth.   Scant stock of dress
Had they to hide the beauties of their forms;
Bright necklaces of berries red as blood,
Sheen bracelets of pied shells, and ankle-bells
Of silver, which they tied on for the dance.
Around their bodies stripéd tunics gleamed,
Leaving their arms and nether members bare
Below the knee—all nude the well-formed feet,
Except the damsel's; she wore sandals soft
Of doeskin; wild flowers ranged in gay festoons
Adorned her waving curls.   And so they danced
And sang and played for many a jocund hour,
In innocence of heart, and void of care.
And more than once, the Virgin, carried away

By her fresh, youthful buoyancy of blood,
Did join them in their merry roundelays,
Dancing and chanting with as light a heart,
As light a foot, as when at Nazareth,
Five years before, she tripped around the well
With all her young companions.
                              When the dance
Was ended, and the tune which gave it life
And rhythmical·being had attained its close,
All rested on the turf in languor sweet,
Conversing of the things before the Flood;
And as they talked, full many an ancient myth,
Full many a sacred history, true as life,
Long dormant in the brain, uprose alive,
With all its epic turns and lyric bursts,
Now moving on in words of home-sweet prose,
Now soaring up on wings of poesy.
Once, Mary seized the maiden's tambourine
(In old times called a timbrel), then began,
In sweetest words of simple narrative,
To tell the children all about the times
When Moses, dry-shod, passed the deep Red Sea,
And of those chariots which moved heavily,
Their dragging wheels struck off—and of the waves
That walled the Hebrews round to right and left—
All the old story, old but ever new;
And when she came to where the chant was sung,
Then Joseph's pilgrim-staff began to beat
In time, his foot to stamp in rhythmic time,
And then uprose in all its early glow,
The oldest song e'er written down in words
Since the creation of this rolling globe,
Mary with voice and clashing timbrel-bells,
With hand accordant and uprisen form,

Sounding the lofty chorus:
            "Sing to the Lord,
    For he hath triumphed gloriously; the horse,
    And eke the horse's rider, hath He thrown
    Deep whelmed beneath the sea."
Like Miriam dancing by the Red seaside,
With strains triumphal 'midst her timbreled throng,
What time the tide at flow came heaving on
O'er the dread wreck-strewn shore, uptossing still
More carcasses with tangled seaweed wreathed,
More broken chariot-wheels, more shattered limbs,
More steeds dead drifting on the moaning flood;
Like Miriam seemed the Virgin as she sang,
And struck high music from the tambourine.
At last the lads and their sweet, black-eyed sister
Rose to go. The Virgin kissed the lass,
And blessed the merry boys, and ere they went
The damsel kissed the Holy Child's sweet lips,
And then they scampered down the steep hillside,
Having in very play imbibed some rays
Of grace divine which blessed them all their lives.
    Beyond the fount a thorny shrub there stood,
With spines and blossoms armed and beautified,
In midst of which a nest was cunningly hid,
Built by a goldfinch. All without 'twas lined
With moss, with lichen, and with woven grass,
Within with hair and wool and swallows' down.
Five young were lodged within its concave cradle,
As yet not fully fledged. Incessant came and went
The careful parents, bringing to their brood
The needful nutriment. The foster-sire,
To please the Child, and show him the sweet ways
Of loving wingéd things, uplifted him
Upon his stalwart shoulder, Atlas-like,

And bade him peep into the blossomed nest,
All guarded round with thorns.   Much was he pleased
To hear the chirping, see the open mouths,
And list the pleasant songs the parents sang
When resting for a moment on the boughs
They raised such tuneful warbling.   Strange it was
To see the Master of Life, enshrined within
An infant's tiny, tender form, and made
Amenable to laws of human growth,
Thus gazing on the things Himself had fashioned,
With all an infant's wonder.
Ere long the Virgin said: "I feel to-day
All wide awake.   Sleep therefore thou a time.
The more the toil, the more the need of rest.
Only that I may pass the interval
More pleasantly, please give me from thy rolls
Of sacred writing, the sweet book of Ruth.
We can not now, I think, be distant far
From where she and Naomi once abode.
This precious lambkin, too, is slumbrous now;
See how he winks his eyes, and smiles like one
Soft lapsing to the heaven of lulling sleep.
Give me the book, I pray, then seek repose."
    He did as she requested.   By the spring
He stretched his limbs along the flowery sward,
And soon was sunk to slumber.   Jesus, too,
Upon his Mother's lap fell deep asleep.
    Then sitting on that lone hill-top, with scroll
As yet unopened in her hand, there came
A meditative mood upon her soul,
Which led her fancy back to times remote,
And bade her spirit brood with dove-like wings
Upon the black chaotic waves which once
Billowed dark-surging o'er the formless void.

Then thought she of the flood, the drifting ark,
The waters rising o'er the highest hills,
Of Noah and his sons, and the long tract
Of intervening time till her own days;
And how from evil good was still evolved,
And how from fields of poisonous bitter weeds,
A charming flower had sprung—and that was Ruth.
From Ruth, the Moabitess, Obed came,
From Obed Jesse, and from Jesse him
Who slew Goliah with a pebble-stone;
Thus link by link the golden chain was forged,
Which drew down God's own essence from above,
To purify the moral atmosphere,
To scathe or heal, to wither or revive.

Then opened she the writing in her hand,
And while the sleepers slumbered 'neath her eye,
And while the goldfinch fed her hungry young,
And while sweet lady-birds sat on her page,
And whilst a distant Pan's pipe tuned the air,
She read, now hushed, now humming to herself,
The sweetest pastoral story ever penned.

And more than once she turned her glance aside
From the old Hebrew words beneath her eye,
To mark the manly form of him who lay
Stretched out among the flowers beside the spring.
Her earthly guide and guardian was he.
How noble looked his features e'en in sleep,
How grand, how innocent, how free from guile,
How fearless and how manly. As a friend
Sent down from heaven she looked upon him then,
And silently thanked heaven for *such* a friend;
And in her inmost heart she felt for him
As she had felt for Holy Gabriel, when
He came t'announce, of all events, the greatest,

The birth of HIM who should renew the world.
A spirit-sympathy united them,
And held them spell-bound in a *golden* world,
Like that which came before the *silver* one,
And banished from their hearts all earthiness,
And placed them in a second Paradise,
An Eden, which moved with them as they moved,
Stood when they stood, and breathed around them airs
From heaven, and bathed them in the lustral founts,
Which flow invisibly from God's own throne,
And drew around them, everywhere they went,
An angel's magic circle, o'er whose bounds
No wanton thought, no evil influence,
Dare for a moment enter.
                              Thus she mused,
And read and mused, in lonely wakefulness,
The dear ones sleeping near her.   Calm and sweet
The minutes followed minutes, till two hours
Had made the shadows longer.   Then her guide,
Refreshed and vigorous, roused himself from sleep,
And soon their wandering commenced anew.

CANTO III.

THE SERPENT.

FOR hours they traveled o'er that border-land,
Half desert and half prairie, till their shadows,
Aye lengthening as the afternoon advanced,
Sloped eastward, growing longer every step.
Joseph, refreshened by his noonday sleep,
And by the bread and wine the children brought them,
And by the holy singing on the hill,
Was blithe beyond his wont.   Like roses glowed

His healthy cheeks, like altar-lights his eyes;
His face at no time was like moon eclipsed
Made somber by earth's shadow—it was like
The sun of spring, which loves to fringe with gold
Or silvery gauze each cloud that intervenes
Between himself and this, our mortal home.
If saintlike ever, then most saintlike he,
When bursting into smiles. The clear-obscure.
Of full-orbed manhood ever made him ready
To weep with those who wept, and laugh with those
Whose hearts o'erflowed with joy. The Mother-maid
Was tempered also thus; e'en when at times
A pensiveness came o'er her, making her droop,
The falling tear quick turned to gleaming pearl;
An infant's laugh, or sudden smile from HIM
Or him, quick brightened up her cheek,
Her eye, and made her full of holy mirth,
Like weeping-elm when sunrise glisters through it,
Or like a weeping willow seen in May,
When passing showers besprinkle it with drops,
And sun and rain contend for mastery.
At last they reached a sandy, circular plain,
More than a score of arrow-flights across
From end to end. Within its center rose
An isolated rock, which seemed as 'twere
A natural pyramid which antique art
Had excavated into halls and rooms,   .
And used it as a temple. Five score feet
Or more it rose above the sandy cirque.
    Thither the travelers wended, both for rest
And water, hoping there to find a spring;
For Joseph had beheld a palm-tree near,
And knew that when on sandy spots that tree
Is seen, a fount is not far off. As onwards

With silent pace they moved, and with slow step,
The hot sun blazing with declining ray,
In horizontal splendor o'er the sand,
It seemed to Joseph like a faint foretaste
Of deserts further south, deserts immense,
Which they were doomed to pass.
                              Reaching the rock,
They found beside its base an olive tree,
A wild one, old and knotty, dry and gnarled,
Whose roots, intwisted in the crevices,
Drew thence their scanty nurture.   The old rock
Had rough, rude steps cut on three sides of it,
Which led respectively to three niched seats,
Affording thus a chance, to those who scaled it,
Of shelter from the sun or driving rain.
Beneath its base upbubbled a scant spring,
Which, trickling onwards, scarce reached eighty yards
Ere it was swallowed up by thirsty sands.
Around the rock, and by the slender rill,
Some spots of green refreshed the eye fatigued,
Some blossoming oleanders, a few brooms,
And one poor, barren fig-tree.   But what most
Caught the lone wanderer's gaze in that wild place,
Was an unmated palm-tree—barren, too.
Add to these plants some twining, prickly stems,
A score of sweetbriers with more spines than flowers,
And a few specimens of that thorny vine
From which, in after years, a crown was woven
For Jesus' holy brow—and you have all—
Save growth of little wild flowers in the grass,
Tiny in size and inconspicuous,
But, when minutely scanned, most beautiful.
Such was the prospect near—but far away,   .
To one upperched upon that airy rock,

North-eastward rose tall mountains veiled in mist
Beyond the lake of Sodom.   Near the rim
Of sand itself were seen, in closer view,
Farms, pasture-lands, and cultivated fields,
And villages on hill-tops.   The strange place,
Ringed as it was with cirques of torrid sand,
And overwaved by streams of heated air,
Reminds us of a scene in the far west,
When Indian hunters, gathered in a group,
Because the kindled prairie is on fire,
Stand on a knoll made bare of prairie-grass,
And feeling thus fire-proof, behold around
The billowy conflagration spreading far.

  Arrived—the ass, unsaddled, was turned loose
To wander 'midst the grass and flowers at will,
When Joseph, swift (for he was smit with thirst),
Took from his traveling-sack a drinking-cup
(A golden cup it was, most rich and bright—
One of the many presents from the kings
Who traveled from the East to see their Lord),
And, placing it some minutes in the spring,
To cool the metal which the sun had warmed,
Bore it, untasted (though half dead with thirst),
To the Madonna, standing 'neath the palm.
Then she, though equally athirst and faint,
With not one drop yet tasted, held it quick
To His lips, whence aye living waters flow,
And ever *shall* flow whilst this earth endures,
And ever after.

    The Holy Infant drank, the Mother drank,
Then gently passed it to the foster-sire,
Who quaffed all that remained—then went for more—
Such sweet, unselfish interchange of love
United those three innocent hearts in one.

Longer this time he loitered by the spring,
Cooling his heated wrists, and culling flowers.
When he returned, how great was his affright,
To view the Virgin Mother, with her face
Turned fountwards, and her eyes uplift to heaven,
Like one in holy trance; whilst by her side,
Somewhat behind her, sported the Child-God,
All fearless on the grass; a monstrous snake
Behind them, vast in bulk, and venomous,
Vibrating a triple tongue, lay there upcoiled,
. All ready for the spring.
Quick, quick as thought, gaining his wonted manhood,
Then Joseph reared his pilgrim's staff aloft,
And striking the poisonous monster on the head,
With one blow dashed its life out. With a start
Then Mary looking suddenly round
Beheld the prostrate snake, upsnatched her child,
And clasped him to her breast, with pallid cheek,
And limbs all over trembling.
   Joseph, meanwhile, having found a fallen branch,
Lifted the ghastly serpent from the ground
In part, in part he trailed it by the brook
(The tail still wreathing with remains of life),
And tossed it in the thorns.
Another brimful cup he then scooped up,
And bade the Blessed Virgin pour it on
His outstretched hands, the which he washed, I ween,
With right good will. The lustral wave, down-poured
By an Immaculate Virgin, did its work
Of cleansing, and, the whilst it did so, he
Thought it a type, a symbol of much good.
And then his trusty pilgrim's staff he laid
Within the brook, some distance from the spring,
Lest one small drop of venom might pollute it,

13

There to be cleansed by holy water's power.
  This done, with one spontaneous act, they both
Knelt on the sward, and both with claspéd hands,
Close side by side, praised God with fervid prayer.
Then up the rock they mounted, step by step,
He bearing in his arms, with tenderest care,
His sacred charge. The ascent was somewhat steep,
Though fraught with little actual danger. Near
The top, they found a cozy seat of stone,
Where comfortably perched, they gazed around
Upon the curious landscape, far and near.
"If I mistake not," said the faithful man,
"Yon peak which melts so softly in the distance,
Is that whereon our holy Moses died,
When from its top he had scanned the Promised Land."
He pointed to the far north-east; she gazed
In silence; thought on thought rolled through her soul,
Almost impictured in her heavenly eyes.
After due time, with gentle voice, she begged him
To end the narrative he had commenced,
Touching the night he spent upon the roof
Of the scarce-finished temple. Willingly
He with her soft request complied, and 'gan
Where he had ended many days before.

CANTO IV.

KEDAR, THE WILD HALF-BREED.

NOT many words he spoke before he spied
  A figure moving fleetly o'er the sands,
And making towards the rock. It was a lad,
Who might have numbered twice seven years perhaps,
Unkempt and wild in his appearance. He

Bestrode a piebald mule, whose springy hoofs
And fine elastic pasterns bore him on,
Wind-swift, across the sand; no saddle had he,
His only bridle-reins, a halter, made
Of firmly-twisted fibers of the palm. '
The mule was painted (all by nature's hand)
With fine fantastic flecks and curious stripes,
Much like a zebra. Bare-armed was the lad,
Bare-legged, bare-footed, with a kerchief red
Wound round his elfish locks; an ostrich-plume
Waved jauntily above his swarthy brow;
A bow of wild-goat's horn was in his hand,
And on his back a well-filled quiver hung.
Sometimes before, sometimes behind him ran
A fleet-foot dog, that seemed of mingled blood,
Half greyhound and half shepherd. Stopping 'neath
The rock, the boy, with ringing shout, called out:
"Hail, father, peace be with thee. Spare my throat
And thine, and coming half-way down the steps,
Pray let us hold a parley at our ease."
    Joseph obeyed; then said the lad, in haste:
"I am in search of mules and asses gone
Astray; since yester eve they wandered off;
Mayhap hast seen them in thy journeying?"
"I have not seen what seemed to be stray mules
Or asses," was the answer. "I must find them,"
The lad replied; "the hunt commenced, must be
Continued. O, the curséd runaways!
Azazel foul confound them. Ha! I see
Thou hast a handsome beast. As white as milk,
With tapering limbs and fine-turned head. What boot"—
Here he laughed merrily—"what boot, what boot?
My mule is almost worth her weight in gold.
O, thou shouldst see her when we hunt gazelles!

Down steepest hills full speed she gallops on,
O'er rolling stones or sliding, slippery sand.
She can outstrip the ostrich. Say, wilt trade?"
"Not I," said Joseph, smiling. "Ishmaelite—
Not so?"   "Not quite," replied the lad; "I am
By some called a wild half-breed, living here
On the edge o' the border-land. My mother was
Born in a tent, and lived for sixteen years
A wanderer o'er the sands. A jolly life!
A wild, aye-roving tent life, that's the life
For me. My father owns a farm-house; he
Takes more delight to doze away his days
Beneath his vines and fig-trees. Thrice a year
He journeys to Jerusalem to pray,
And offer sacrifice, and free-will offerings,
And tithes, and firstlings of the flock and field.
Tell me, dost know the name of yonder fount?"
"Indeed I do not," answered Joseph; "tell *me*."
"The Fount of Halves. Twelve hours it runs, and twelve
Ebbs down to nothing; nay, more; half the year
It flows in this half-wise and half goes dry.
A niggard fountain-head it may be called.
No wonder here a barren olive stands,
A barren fig-tree there, a barren palm
Yonder. Good heavens! there's something glittering there
Beside the spring. A drinking-cup. Ho! ho!
How beautiful! Pure gold, pure gold—how rich!"
    Whereat he slid flash-quick down from his mule,
Seized the rich prize, and eyed it round and round.
Gazing upon it swift without, within;
Then dipped it in the spring, and drank, and gazed,
And gazed and drank again with deep delight.
    "Whence came it?" then he asked, with eagerness.
"Was it the work of sprites in some far land

Nearer the rising sun? Its work embossed
Enchants me, and I dream of something strange
And new, and wonderful beyond all thought.
Magical—magical, ay, that's the word.
I've heard strange stories told beside the fire
At night by camel drivers, when they pause
To rest upon the sands; stories most strange,
Of genii and enchanters, far renowned,
Who, by their skill, make things of potent charm,
Which even spirits obey. Is this one of
Those wonder-working talismans? But, no,
My foolish fancy oft leads me astray.
'Tis a rich drinking cup, and nothing more.
Now listen, stranger, I will give you for it
My mule, my dog, my bow, my ostrich plume,
All that I have, for this *one* drinking-cup.
Come, come! that's fair. Say, wilt thou trade for it?"
  "Not for all these, and all your father owns
Besides in land, in flocks, in herds, in grain,
With ten times more added to the full sum,
And ten times ten times all owned by the tribe
From which your mother sprang, could all this be
Massed in one heap, and all that heap increased,
By some strange magic power, a hundred-fold,
I would not let you have that drinking-cup.
'Tis worth more than its weight, as men say, *in gold.*
It has a history belonging to it."
  "Do tell me that strange history," said the lad;
"I'd give my mule to hear it."
  "I dare not tell it," was the quick reply.
"Not? Then the swiftest and the cunningest
Shall bear it off as prize." And as he spoke
He vaulted on his mule, with cup in hand,
And, standing upright on the creature's back,

As does a clown in some equestrian cirque,
He held it up with archly winking face,
In which sly roguery and daring fun
Were blended equally, then slipt adown
Into his seat, and shouting to the mule,
Off like the wind he scampered.   Bowshots two
In length he raced along the sands, then wheeled,
And posting back with the same madcap pace,
Just 'neath the spot where Joseph stood, drew rein.
Again he stood up clown-like on the beast,
Which stopt as still as any marble mule,
And on his face were pictured curiously
Commingled moods and swiftly-passing trains
Of varying emotions, shifting ever:
Whim, fun, deep inborn gift of thievery,
Sucked in with mother's milk; and mixed with these,
A trace or two of pious reverence
(Perhaps caught from his father).
He waved the cup aloft and said aloud:
" How easy even now this cup were mine.
Behold yon wooded hills skirting the south,
I know each winding glen and narrowing gorge,
And every cave and hiding-place among them,
Where sheltering I might lurk, and thence might reach
The pathless wilderness.   This thing would then
Be mine, and Kedar, all the rest of life,
Most rich in flocks and herds.   The sale of this
Would give me wherewithal to purchase mares
Of purest Arab blood, and domedaries,
And tents and wives, and make me, ere my death,
Like one of those rich patriarchs that we read of,
Who lived in olden times, as tells the Book.
With *such* a start, wealth like the wealth of Job,
Would soon pour in.   *Now*, Kedar 's a poor lad,

With naught but mule and dog and dancing plume,
With goathorn bow and quiver; poor, but honest—
Poor Kedar! honest, simple-hearted Kedar."
 This saying, with tears and laughter strangely mixed,
He held the cup aloft, and Joseph, stepping
Down the stone stairs, placed in his hand a coin
Of shining gold, and on his head his hand
He laid, and blessed him thrice with eyes upraised.
The boy, with look subdued and eyelash sunk,
Received the kindly blessing; then he wiped
A trickling tear from off his tawny cheek,
And once again dismounted from his mule,
While Joseph step by step slow journeyed upwards.
Kedar with quick eye glanced from him to the top,
And viewing there, enthroned in upper air,
A female form (young Kedar's eyes were keen,
Nay, almost telescopic in their power)
And seeing there the loveliest face unveiled
That ever yet his eye had lit upon,
His orient fancy, kindling to full glow,
Took her for spirit dropt from highest heaven,
And when, as in a trance he saw her gazing
Far, far away across the sands, across
The stagnant waters of the Sea of Death,
With eye fixed on the Mount where Moses died,
Kedar no longer could withstand—he sank
Upon his tawny knees and worshiped her.
This was the turning-point in Kedar's life.
Glance we a moment at his after years
As vision represents them to the view.
The touch of Joseph's hand, his deep-toned voice,
His blessing and his prayer commenced the change,
And drove some evil demons from his breast;
Then, the remembrance of an honest deed,

Of a temptation nobly overcome,
Soothed his whole being with a joy ne'er felt
Before in his wild life; good feelings took
The place of wicked ones expelled; and then
The sight of that all-lovely Lady on
The Mount, built up the keystone of the arch
Of his conversion from a semi-savage
To a true, honest man.   Soon all his ways
Were other than they had been, all his thoughts.
His father, seeing the happy change commenced,
Did all he could to foster it.   He sold
His frontier farm and traveled to the north;
With joy he left the reckless borderland,
And settled in the quiet hill-country
Not many miles from Hebron.
                      Kedar there
Became in time a husbandman so true,
So honest, upright, and so holy-hearted,
That all men far and near respected him.
For wife he gained a pious Hebrew maid
Untainted by a drop of Ishmael's blood,
Who loved him better than she loved herself,
And bore him every other year a son
Until they counted six, six blooming boys.
Then every other year she bore a daughter,
Until *they* numbered six—the sixth her last.
All comely-featured, eastern-eyed brunettes,
With arching eyebrows and a rich-hued skin,
Six yellow peaches, all with cheeks of red.
And thus his charming flock was full, complete,
Twelve by the count, and twelve upon his heart,
Like the twelve jewels on the High-priest's breast.
They were in fact to him twelve little stars,
The lovely zodiac of his household heaven.

When he had reached his seven and fortieth year,
Kedar, as was his wont, with all the twelve,
Went to Jerusalem to celebrate
The Passover. His ample tent he pitched
On holy Olivet on a high point,
From which a spacious prospect on all sides
Expanded to the view, the city seen
Across the brook of Kedron, holy Mount
Of Zion, and the Temple on Moriah,
All bright and hallowed objects to the eye,
And on the other side the salt Dead Sea.
  One day, a memorable day for him,
He saw the Lord of Life and Light, enshrined
In human flesh. Then grew the change complete.
The wild, light-fingered rover of the sands,
Who had once borne the holy cup away,
And had returned it, changing ever still,
Now found the consummation of that change
Complete and most delighful. How HIS words
Refreshed, like morning dew, his open heart;
How, as he heard them, did his spirit burn
Within him, as if live coals from the altar,
With holiest incense mingled, kindled him,
And made him long for heaven!
                              HIS words he heard,
Beheld His miracles, believed His power,
Received His blessing, and was blessed indeed.
The Savior's twelve felt often not too proud
To sing and pray with *his*, and when he left
The Olive Mount and reached his happy home,
It seemed a holier home to all of them—
A holier and a sweeter. Counting then,
He counted one by one the starry twelve,
And lo! not one was lost. Here let us pause,
The coming canto needs a brain refreshed.

CANTO V.

THE TWO JOSEPHS.

AN isolated hill it was, at first
Rising sharp-pointed from the cirque of sand,
A sort of natural obelisk, the work
Of spent volcanic forces weird and wild,
By Superstition's hand in after years
Changed in appearance; this had carved those steps
Rude winding upward, flattened its peaked top,
And made it look, to one who from below
Viewed it, a rude truncated pyramid
Devoted to dark rites and Pagan gods.
A half a score of paces from the top
An excavated chamber might be seen,
Rotunda-shaped, with dome-like vault above,
Marked over with inscriptions old and dim,
In unknown characters and pictures rude.
Of these, one form was oftentimes repeated,
A female head, arched with a belt of stars,
And having on her front a crescent moon.
    When twilight 'gan to darken into night
Joseph lit up his torch, and stepping in
The antique chapel, viewed it round and round,
And found it empty quite, quite hushed and still.
Assured that all was safe, he straightway led
The Virgin in, and showed her all the place
By torchlight.   Much she shuddered when at first
She viewed those mystic letters, half erased,
Like those inscribed upon the Moab Stone
Which modern brains have recently unlocked;
And much the Blessed Virgin feared at first
Lest something all-unholy haunted there,
Making that round fane frightful.   But when he
Who acted as her pilot and her guide,

Assured her it was safe and free from harm,
And pointed to a little open platform
Three steps below, where he would make his couch,
Thus intercepting danger from the earth,
She gave her glad consent to slumber there.

 With care he spread her pictured carpet down
Near the fane's center, ranged her pillows soft,
And having fixt the lighted torch securely
In an old fissure in the rock, he read
A portion of the Holy Word, and sang
And prayed, and prayed and sang again,
Then leaving there the torch to cheer the place,
He bade her sweet good night, adding that he
Would mount to the summit of the obelisk
Like watchman on his watch-tower, to survey
The concave heavens above, the earth beneath.

 As sleep oftimes appears to mimic Death,
In its deep quiet and passivity,
So, like its stronger brother, it is wont
To wrap its limbs in other garbs than those
Which waking life assumes. In linen fresh
And fragrant, white and pure, she robed her form,
Too loose t' impede the blood, and sprinkled o'er
With aromatic drops,
Ottar of roses and sweet lavender,
To make her slumber balmier; then she couched
Her form for rest, soft clasped her virgin palms,
And breathed another prayer in dulcet words:
 "Eternal Father of the universe,
In thy hands I resign thy Son and mine.
I know Thou wilt protect Him from all harm;
And this, thy humble handmaid, shield her too.
Here in the center of this antique fane,
Once on a time the site of rights impure,

I lay me down to rest. Oh, keep away
All evil spirits; let them not come near;
Let no malific influence infect
The air we breathe, or poison holy sleep."
    "*Sleep,*" then, was echoed softly from the east,
"*Sleep,*" softer still, re-echoed from the west;
And then she knew that angel guards were near,
And laid her down to rest. With thoughts firm fixed
On heavenly contemplations, down she lay
Until through seas of slumber sinking down,
Aye deeper down, she lost all sense of earth,
And slept like ring-dove nestling 'mid the rocks.
    Ascend we now with Joseph ten steps higher,
And gaze around above us. Earth was dark,
And melancholy all her voices. Owls
Screeched from the woods; foxes, with sharp, shrill bark,
Untuned the ear of night; hyenas moaned
Like wailing infants; watch-dogs howled from far;
The distant Dead Sea glimmered in the moon,
Who now showed half her face; scant lights were seen
From villages remote and lone hill-tops,
Making the darkness ghastlier.
               Such the scene
On earth. But in the heavens, the concave vault,
From zenith down to the horizon's verge,
All round and round, as far as vision reached,
Was all ablaze with splendor. Joseph's eye,
Accustomed all his life to splendid nights,
Had never viewed one half so glorious.
Three planets were in sight: Mars in the east,
New risen, fresh, ruddy, rayed with lashes red;
Venus, slow sinking, silvery, and mild;
High Jupiter, imperial overhead,
Near whom the starry Sickle hung in heaven,

As though an angel harvester had ceased
To cut the harvests of the worlds, and left
His reap-hook gleaming on the Lion's mane,
Such heavenly peace was symbolized above.
   Long Joseph, spellbound by the glorious view,
In silence gazed above him: Earth appeared
So dark, so dreary, and the heavens so bright,
So gorgeous, that a yearning came upon him
('Twas but for one short moment) to leave all
Most treasured here below, and (if he could)
To wing his journey starward. Soon this wish,
As something sinful, was expelled;
                    —And, lo!
Looking around, he saw close by his side
A glorious angel standing. A bright crown,
Gleaming with diamond and with chrysolite,
With emerald, and with opal, girt his brow,
Like Ariadne's starry diadem;
Beneath its cirque, ringlets of custering curls
Over his shoulders waved, and down his back.
Glossed and eye-spotted, like the gorgeous bird,
Fabled to draw the car of Juno, were
His ample wings, loose-folded, mantling all
His length of stature; an internal light
Not dazzling, but of softest tempered glow,
Like the mild splendor of the milky-way,
Invested him—as when a spirit-lamp
Burns, shaded of its glare, within the round
Of a transparent lantern, rainbow-hued.
His countenance expressed benignity
And sweetness, beautifully blended with
Vigor and courage. Smiling, he began,
   " Be not so startled, Joseph. By thy side
Stands one who once was mortal like thyself,

And bore the self-same name.
I too went down to Egypt, as thou knowest
From having often read the Holy Book.
With Medianitish merchantmen I went
Across long deserts on a camel's back,
With freights of myrrh and balm and spicery
Slow journeying to the Nile.   The tale, though true,
Sounds like the wild romances Arabs tell
At night around their camp-fires.   After death,
My spirit rose to Him who made me.   I
Inhabit now the New Jerusalem, ·
Where one day thou shalt see me.   As on earth,
In heaven I mounted from a lower grade
Forever higher upwards in the scale
Of being—still expanding—still ascending—
Among the ranks of angels.   I have come
To talk with thee upon this pyramid
As spirit talks with spirit, when the one
Is prisoned in the bars of mortal flesh,
And th' other ranges free through airy space
Untrammeled, unimpeded.
                              I have come
Commissioned earthward by the Power Supreme,
In simple words such as man speaks to man,
To tell thee that thy late heroic deed,
When thou didst slay the serpent, has been seen
With admiration by the heavenly host,
And by the spirits of the universe.
It was an Evil Demon that informed
The body of that snake,—not Satan's self,
But an inferior devil aping Satan,
One smit with pride Satanic, who thus hoped
To consummate what Satan had begun.
The *body* he assumed thou didst destroy,

The bestial *soul* still wanders o'er the earth,
Watching his opportunity. Fear not;
The hosts of heaven are now on the alert;
Hell and its legions shall not harm the Babe,
Or the Babe's mother, or his foster-sire.
But be thyself still watchful. What thy arm
Accomplishes on earth in His defense,
Shall all be written in the books of Heaven,
And all shall be rewarded.
                              I have come
Also to give thine eye a passing glimpse
Of stellar glories which thou shalt behold
Some future day with vision spiritual,
Unclouded, unobscured. Long centuries
Shall roll across thy birth-star, ere the truths
I now impart in confidence, shall be
Discovered and believed by mortal men.
Each truth, when time is ripe for it, shall burst
Its muffling mask, and fill the earth with light
And joy and sense of power progressive. First
Thy promise I exact, not to divulge
What, more by hasty glimpses than by long,
Laborious study, I shall now impart.
Yet even these, imperfect though they be,
May give thee some enjoyment, foretaste sweet
Of coming ecstasies, when thou art free
To range on spirit-wings from world to world.
Wilt promise me?"
                      "With all my heart and soul;
Time's secrets, well I know, await their turn;
The birth of the oncoming centuries
Must not be hurried; morning's teeming womb,
In halcyon calmness undisturbed, must rest
Till birth-time be matured. But tell me, pray,

Shall *she*, the partner of my wanderings,
Companion of my flight o'er desert sands,
Remain ungifted with those lofty truths,
One glimpse of which brings gladness?   From the *world*
I willingly conceal such treasured thought,
From *her* to hide it would be fraught with pain."
  Then, smiling sweet, the heavenly Joseph spoke:
"Such hard condition hath not been imposed,
Believe me, by the Almighty Sire of all.
Freely as is thy wont thou mayst converse
With her, the partner of thy wanderings,
To whom in spirit-wedlock thou art bound
In sanctity and chasteness.   Far as words
Can body thought and waft it to the mind,
Thou art at liberty to tell her all.
'Twill separate you two from all the world
More sacredly.   On this high spirit-peak
You two may stand, and interchange sweet thoughts
Together, like two disembodied souls,
Conversing on the wonders yet untried
Of worlds on worlds unnumbered.   Such high lore
Ennobles, elevates, and purifies.
'Tis meet that those who educate God's Son,
Should have their souls expanded and enwinged
More than the souls around them."
                                Joseph bowed,
Like one assenting to the words of him
With whom he talks, and silent waits for more.
  "Know first," continued then the angel bland,
"This little earth thou liv'st on, and to which
Thou shalt consign thy bones, is a small sphere,
Which we, the wingéd ones, can compass round
Ere from an hour-glass twenty sands can fall.
Spheroid in form, with liquid fire within,

With a small band of sister-spheres it wheels
In an elliptic pathway round the sun.
Two of these sisters I will show you now.
Look through this optic tube. 'Twas made in heaven
By my directions and at my command,
With fixtures fitted to a mortal eye,
And carefully stored up for future use."
   Then pointing it toward the darkened west
Where the fair planet Venus, not yet set,
Still trembled on the horizon's brink, the angel bland
Arranged it without effort, lightning-quick,
And bade the mortal look. He looked with joy—
"What see'st thou through the optic tube?"
                              "I see
What in appearance seems a fair half-moon,
With mountains and with valleys of its own,
A lovely world complete and full of life,
One half illumined soft, and one half hid:
Oh, how my spirit pants to visit it."
"That mayhap thou may'st do," was the reply,
"When thou hast burst thy fleshly wrappings; now
Far other pilgrimage awaits thee."
   Next pointing to the disk of ruddy Mars,
He said, "Behold the planet which the Greeks
Name from the god of war. The Arabs too
Adore him as a warlike deity,
Calling him Nergal: blood-red fanes to him
They consecrate, and garments wet with blood;
His statue in one hand holds a red sword,
And in the other a dissevered head:
Thus superstition mounts up to the stars,
Disfiguring them with fables."
                        "Oh, how calm
He looks," said Joseph, "calm and bright in heaven!
14

What long red lustrous rays shoot round his orb!
How beautiful!   The clouds which flash around
The setting sun not splendider in tint,
The morning-red not brighter.   Hail, all hail,
Thou glad companion of my own birth-star!
Oh, how I long to wing my way to thee,
And plunge into thy rosy atmosphere.
But tell me, hallowed angel, why appear
His poles so flushed with fire ? "
                    "Vast heaps of ice,"
Answered the angel, "gathering there, reflect
The sun.   Cold things are sometimes bright.   Behold,
His north pole has commenced with heat to melt,
His south to freeze into an ampler curve,
Up-piling high its frozen battlements,
Gleaming with glow antarctic."
                    "Oh, strange, strange!
What I supposed was lovely flame at play
In roseate splendor, is a mount of ice.
I feel like one who thought to grasp a rose
And pricks him with a thorn.   The denizens
Of that fair planet, tell me, do they suffer
A greater cold than we ? "
                    "The Sovereign Sire
Hath moulded them with nicest skill," replied
The courteous angel, "and with kindliest care
Hath fashioned them to love their ruddy home.
With genial warmth bland summer gladdens now
The northern temperate zone; the southern, with
Bright hearths and hospitable fires they warm,
Thawing frore winter through the shortened day,
And with high festivals and jocund sports
Making the long night joyous.   Few worlds are
More happy or more splendidly contrived,

Few in its days and years, and in its climes,
Resemble more our own. But let us shift
The starry scene: behold another world!"
    He pointed straight the tube to Jupiter,
And cried, "Now mark the so-called Jovian star;
What seest thou? Speak."
                    "A larger world of wonder,
All circumzoned with curious belts and bands,
Larger, but not so red. To me it seems
More distant from the sun. Between the belts
Methinks I can see mountain-tops and plains,
All dimly—dimly. Moons? what lovely moons!
One? two? three? No—yes—one is darkening now,
And sinking in eclipse. Another now
Is rising out of shadow! Glorious sight!
Like our own moon she seems when she upclimbs
Above the billowy sea.
Another still far out in distant space
Like finest pin's-point twinkling. Four in all?"
    "Four moons in all. Thou hast discerned aright."
"Four handmaids seem they," said the musing man,
"All waiting on their lord; some with their veils
Uplifted; some with faces muffled close,
Advancing or receding round their king
In sweet quaternion dance that never tires."
    "Well hast thou caught the glory of the scene,"
Said the grand spirit, smiling. "Many a time
Has this small globe called earth wheeled round the sun,
Since I, imprisoned in a frame of flesh,
Was governor of Egypt. Then I sat
On my high chariot, like a rolling throne,
And moving through the streets on golden wheels,
With footmen racing in the front and rear,
And pluméd cavalry on either side,

In Memphis or in hundred-gated Thebes,
Crowds thronging bowed the knee and cried aloud,
' *Hail, Savior of the world!* '   Then, in my piide,`
I vainly thought no scene could equal this,
For glory and for splendor.   Not so now.
What thou hast just beheld is grander far,
And more ennobling.   The comparison
Between the two, 'tis this that makes me smile,
And eke thy childlike wonder."
                                   Like the glow
Of summer morning smiled the angel then,
Looking with pleased attention on the man.
As when some grand astronomer, large-brained,
Calm-breasted, full of starry thoughts,
And also full of kindly feelings, sees
His curly-headed boy among his tubes,
His maps, his quadrants, compasses, and globes,
And smiling, lifts him up to take a peep
Through the *big telescope*, as mayhap once
The elder Herschel did his prattling son
(Since grown illustrious), showing him with glee
Some dread volcanic mountain in the moon,
Or some fine star, which to the naked eye
Seems single, doubled through the magic tube,
Thus kindly smiled the angel on the man.
"One planet more I fain would show thee still,"
Said then the angel, wrapt in calm regard,
" But have not now the power.   Before the third
Watch of the present night is passed, 'twill not
Arise to view—ere which I must away.
Oft sent on missions through the universe,
I have upon its glorious orb alit,
By day and night, and circled round its sphere.
Full thirty of earth's years compose its year;

So long its orbit, and so slow its course
Around our sun; its day is less than half;
So quick, with all its bulk, it spins around
On its own axis. In the Latin tongue
'Tis called Saturnus. With your present form
You could not live or breathe upon its orb,
So far off from the sun, so strange its air,
So wonderful its climate and its soil.
Behold yon picture."
         At a sign from him
Another angel instant floated down,
A rosy form, dim-bright, and flutter-winged,
And placed within the mortal's hand a scroll
Impictured with the picture of a world,
More wonderful than any yet beheld.
   "You see before you," the kind spirit said,
"A sun in little, with eight little worlds,
And three concentric rings. Behold those moons!
One is now rising, one is setting now;
One from eclipse is heaving, darkening one;
One culminates; one touches the mid-point
Between the horizon's verge and zenith; one
Half-orbed appears, one full. Behold the rings,
How grandly round the globe they curving gleam
With strange illumination."
         Though entranced
With what he saw, here Joseph's eyelids closed,
And Palinurus-like, who gazed so long
Upon the Pleiads, Hyads, and the Pole,
That he could gaze no more and fell asleep,
So, from o'erstrained attention, Joseph slept.
   An hour he slumbered. Then the o'ertasked brain
Awoke refreshed. The angel still was there.
His instrument was resting where it stood.

He spake these words: "Soon must I leave thee, Joseph.
E'en should the knowledge thou hast gained to-night
Appear to fade away in part, and leave
Imperfect traces of itself behind,
As soon as death shall disenthrall thy spirit,
That knowledge shall revive and reappear
In fresher, livelier colors. E'en through life,
Much, much shall stay with thee through all thy days,
To brighten and enlarge thy mind, and make
Thee happier. Oft delicious glimpses shall
Flash on thee from the glories thou hast seen,
Immersing thee in rapture; oft on nights
To come, shalt thou upon the desert wastes,
The whilst the stars are glittering overhead,
Draw pictures with thy staff upon the sands,
Circles, ellipses, planispheres, and cones,
And pointing first to desert, then to sky,
Explain heaven's mysteries as best thou canst,
To *her* who is the pole-star of thy life."
He paused and waved his hand. A moment more
Both instrument and spirit disappeared.
The mortal, so it seemed, stood all alone.
Such solitude, after *such* company,
Oppressed and weighed him down; so he resolved
To find his preappointed sleeping place,
And rest till morning.
                Passing by the fane,
Where the blessed Virgin lay, with timid step
He entered in, beheld the torch still burning,
Beheld the Mother and the Child asleep;
Ottar of roses sweetened all the air,
And lavender, from aromatic hills,
Perfumed the carved rotunda; there they lay,
So innocent, so pure, so beautiful,

The Virgin, and the Virgin's Child, asleep.
Then Joseph knelt adown in silent prayer,
Turning his gaze to those so softly sleeping.
Of all that he had seen and heard that night,
This vision touched him most.   He smiled, he wept,
He was awe-struck, enraptured.   Scarce possessed
Of power to tear himself away, he knelt
In that same reverent posture minutes blest,
Thinking in that short time a world of thoughts,
Prayer in his heart, and silence on his lips,
Adoring, gazing, wrapt in holy trance.
Then slowly, softly creeping down the steps,
Those trinal steps which downward led him, on
To where a platform carved from solid rock
O'erhung the side of that old pyramid,
He stretched his limbs to slumber, gazing on
The stars, until his lids were closed in sleep.

CANTO VI.

THE LOVE-FEAST ON THE MOUNT.

FULL many a star arose and many set,
  From hour to hour throughout the holy night,
And still the Virgin lay in dreamless rest,
And if dreams came at all, they, bubble-like,
Floated adown the noiseless stream of sleep
Unheeded, unremembered.   But when dawn
Sent her first messengers around the east,
A vision came, gift of her guardian angel,
Which filled her brain with splendor.
                              She beheld
A heavenly spirit on a floating car
Of roseate cloud, who thus addressed her: "Wake,

Mary, awake.   Another day will soon
Rise o'er the earth, and thou must journey far
Ere sunset.   Thy tired pilot slumbers still;
For he, great part of the past night, was wrapt
In high communion with a holy angel,
Concerning secrets of the world of stars.
Some centuries agone, this antique dome
Where thou hast slumbered was a noted fane,
Where rites reputed holy were performed,
And where a priestess lived both day and night.
On th' east side of this circular room there is
A secret door, which opens inwardly
On a short passage, leading to a bath,
Which in old times was kept in good repair,
And fed by cisterns filled with rain-water,
Stored there for instant use.   For many an age
These works had been neglected; but last night
By angel-hands the cisterns were replaced
By others new and clean, and angel-hands,
In golden buckets, bore from melting clouds
Good store of purest water.   Hie thee there,
Madonna blest, ere sunrise; bathe thy limbs;
Refresh them with sky-water sweet and cool;
Then bathe the Holy Child."
                              Mary arose ·
And did as the Sweet Vision ordered her,
And found the lavatory all complete,
And turned a little spile fixed on a tube,
And saw the lucid waters gushing out
As sweet as when they left the melting clouds.
    She bathed and was refreshed.   Then, tracing back
Her buoyant steps, she bore the Holy Child
To the same spot, and bathed his blooming limbs,
Till, like a rosebud moist with morning dew,

The sweet grew sweeter, fresh grew fresher still,
And the pure human body, miniature shrine
Of Godhead, gleamed within the wave
Like to a delicate-tinted water-lily
Emerging from a lake. Oh, then they felt
So happy both, so joyous, so refreshed!
   Then out she peeped to see how Joseph fared,
And found him wrapped in slumber undisturbed,
With arms soft-folded crosswise on his breast,
And face which e'en in sleep was starward turned,
As if, star-gazing, he had sunk to rest.
The shelf on which he slept, with dizzy poise
Hung o'er a dangerous depth; but there he lay
The image calm of slumbrous quietude,
Breathing so regular and rhythmical,
That well she knew his pulse beat healthily.
   Some lilies of a new and lovelier kind
Than any she had ever seen before
Were scattered up and down along the steps—
Those three fair sloping steps, which, mystic-wise,
Led from the rounded chamber where *she* slept
To where her Pilot rested airily.
She knew not whence those wondrous lilies came,
Or what they meant—she only knew how sweet,
How heavenly sweet they smelt, how pure they looked,
How snow-white and immaculate they were.
Elastic, to the hill-top next she tripped,
Bearing the Holy Infant in her arms,
And long stood gazing on the dawning scene,
Stars fading, morn advancing—a faint rim
Of delicate red, with here and there a break,
Clasping the horizon circle-wise and soft,
E'en as she clasped her treasure. Far north-east,
Fogs heavy-dark o'erhung the torpid lake

Called the Dead Sea, as if a sable band
Of black death-angels had outspread their plumes
To hide its horror from the coming dawn,
And cover up with dusk Tartarean veils
The very site where, in the days of old,
Stood Sodom and Gomorrah.
　　　　　　　　　　On the brink
Long she stood gazing.　When she turned her face,
Lo! on that natural pyramid she saw
A dainty table spread, and all inlaid
With costliest gems, and rare mosaic work,
Like that which, in the land where Arno flows,
Is called "pietra dura."　Lions' paws,
In number four, ended four golden legs
On which the table stood; four golden beaks,
Like those of eagles, formed the upper parts;
Symbolic griffons these—the types of strength
And swiftness—types of lordliness on earth
And of dominion in the upper air.
　　She saw not, knew not, by what unseen hands
That table had been wafted from afar.
Achilles' fabled shield, by Vulcan framed,
Contained upon its round, of pictured scenes
A greater number crowded in small space,
But not more beautiful in workmanship,
Or more suggestive of swift-thronging thoughts.
　　There Paradise was pictured.　There appeared
The rivers four which through the Garden flowed;
The encircling mountains towering up so high;
The angel watchers on the mountain top;
There our first parents in successive scenes—
Adam, in that grand moment, when he sprang
To life, all perfect from the Maker's hand,
And saw a world around, above, beneath,

All beautiful, all new: the birth of Eve,
Adam's full rapture and Eve's wonderment;
Their nuptial arbor, their espousals pure;
Their fragrant garden-work at dawn of day
Among fresh flowers and overarching vines;
Their walks by moonlight over dewy hills;
Their rambles through long woodland avenues
At quiet eventide; their orisons
On bended knees, with hand in hand enclasped;
Their sweet repasts, with angels for their guests;
Their noontide slumbers under fanning palms,
With lions sleeping round, and spotted pards,
And elephants; such charming scenes, in short,
As the Miltonic muse in after days,
In words more vivid than an artist's pencil,
Depictured to the life.

               Not to the fall,
Temptation and sad fall, extended they;
That darkening view of Eden was not there;
Nothing but life and joy and innocence,
Confiding love, and mutual, pure esteem.

   Mary immaculate stood long entranced
Above the table's polished, pictured round,
And read the pictures as we read a book.
The Infant Saviour too, young as he was,
Appeared to understand much that he saw,
And pointing now at this and then at that,
He looked at Eve and called her "his mamma;"
And when he viewed her with her tresses long
At work among the flowers, or standing by
A lakelet's brink (her image mirrored there)
He clapt his little hands and crowed for glee.
Then down she tript to where, upon the rock,
Her pilot and her mortal guardian slept,

And with a bird-like carol, soft and sweet,
She strove to rouse him gently. By degrees
The dulcet music reached his sleep-sealed brain,
And mingling pleasingly with his own dreams,
Caused him to smile and utter silly words,
Joining disjointed phantasies together,
Whereat she laughed, and sang, and laughed again,
And said: "Such madcap phrases ill agree,
Methinks, with a land-pilot's dignity."
A spice of girlishness thus seasoned oft
Her frolic words and ways, like blooming flowers
Around the statue of a worshiped saint.

    Joseph at last awoke, and knew at once
Her cause of mirth. She told him of the bath,
And of the table on the high hill-top,
And of its wondrous pictures. Much amazed,
He did at once as she instructed him,
And in due time returned, refreshed and cooled,
When, both ascending to the highest point
Of that strange mount, they saw the table there,
On the same spot, but not now bare of food;
For, on its pictured surface now appeared
Plates, goblets, spoons, and knives, and chalices
Of gold, and in their proper vessels, bread,
Some dainty bits of savory meat, and eggs;
And for their drink pure water from fresh springs,
Deep underground (by spirits fetched from thence),
And to give richer zest to the repast,
A tiny cup stood by the plate of each,
Filled with some aromatic cordial,
Extract perhaps of that Arabian berry,
Now known and prized, and used both east and west,
With balmiest spices flavored.

    Aye, as the blissful feast was going on,

Did one or other, with supreme delight,
Lift up a plate or vessel and behold
The pictured figures that adorned the same,
Suggestive of the age of gold, or calling up
In fancy man's primeval happiness,
His purity and innocence:
A herd of antlered deer, a flock of birds
Circling in rapture round the woman's head,
Swans, silver-white, disporting on clear lakes,
Peacocks, with all their painted plumes unfurled,
Fair birds of Paradise upon the wing,
Flying against the spicy breeze, or perched
On airiest palms, or that still lovelier bird,
With twelve outbranching feathers in its tail,
And two more, fashioned like an antique lyre,
Hence called the Lyre-bird, found in far-off isles
Of th' utmost orient. (Often did the CHILD
Admire this gorgeous fowl, and often count
The feathers in the fan-like tail outspread.)
Then there were gentle antelopes asleep
Between maned lions' paws, a snowy lamb
Licking a tiger's uncontracted claws,
And all creation, tree, and stream, and beast,
At peace! at peace!
Thus Joseph and the Virgin sat at meat,
And feasted charmingly upon the height.
    And ever and anon ambrosial airs
Played round them, sporting with fair Mary's locks,
And blowing Christ's into more graceful curves,
Airs fresh from heaven, or wafted round them soft
By plumes invisible: airs novel now
And never known on earth; now, earthly-sweet,
Such as in springtide eastern gardens waft,
Sweet breath of myrrh, or modest mignonette,

Or orange, rose, vanilla, tuberose,
Or beds of fresh-blown pansies.
    Thus Joseph and pure-hearted Mary sat
And feasted charmingly upon that mount.
    Not Adam's self and Eve before the fall
Ever partook a banquet with more joy,
Or thanked the Giver with a warmer heart.
Not by set words of thanks, spoke parrot-wise
And mumbled out with artificial drawl,
They thanked Him; but by gayety of heart,
By larklike upward mounting of the soul,
By warm benevolence to all mankind,
By silent bursts of prayer heard but by God,
By clear pure-heartedness, and by the love
They bore each other, and their Present Lord,
They thanked Him constantly, through all the feast.
    A love-feast, was it? Feast of love indeed!
Immaculate Mary never looked more gay,
More merry-hearted, rosy-cheeked, more pure,
With now and then a flight of innocent wit,
Like a light arrow, feathered, but unbarbed,
Blown by some gay child through a hollow reed,
To fondle with the wind, and which ofttimes
Is wafted backwards to the rosy mouth
Which had propelled it.
              So they sat at meat,
And feasted with their LORD upon the mount.
    To close the banquet, each then, sip by sip,
Drank from the cup prepared by angel-hands
For their refreshment—cordial of bland power—
And as the aromatic liquid spread
Its soft, diffusive glow along their nerves,
And gradual through the brain, the soul itself
Was gently, blandly influenced by the draught,

And in serener mood, with steadier thrill,
Became still more conceptive than before,
More keen, more smooth, more active, more becalmed,
And (strange to tell) more dreamy-wide-awake.
Then Joseph, in fine mood for it, began
Again to tell that curious mystic dream,
Which he the eve before would have commenced,
Had not young Kedar's advent called him off.
That dream, like Delos, had been floating loose
Upon his memory, drifting to and fro,
Like Delos, which, as classic poets tell,
Was birthplace of the twins, Apollo bright,
And Artemis, the silver-shafted Queen;
Like Delos, isle afloat upon the sea.
Many a year the vivid vision waved
Before his spirit, brighter now, now dimmer,
Varying in shape, in substance still the same,
That oft he doubted whether 'twere a dream,
Or something witnessed by his waking eyes.
'Twas called "The Seven Spirits of the Rainbow,
Seen in a Vision on the Temple's Top."
Now, all his doubts were solved. During the night
The dream had reappeared. In all its freshness
It came back to him for the second time
With all its imagery, its lyric bursts,
Its music and its sights; it came again,
And now the floating isle became the fixed.
   Then Joseph told the vision. Like a seer
Or prophet of the olden days he told it;
But we, for lack of time, must pass it by,
Or fold it on its shelf for future use,
If called for. Mayhap no one cares for it.
If so, it may in darkness rest, to kindle
A Christmas fire upon some future year,

And help to cheer that joyous holiday.
When he had finished, Mary thanked him sweet,
But he, for recreation, played with Christ.
As some flight-happy pigeon wings its way
To a near bubbling fountain-head to drink,
Or to a meadow streamlet, there to bathe
And purify its painted plumes, and play,
Scattering the water-drops around like pearls,
So Joseph to the fountain-head repaired
Of all man's renovation and delight.
He played with Christ.   O, sweet disport indeed!
He bore him on his shoulders round the mount
Three times, and pointed out the far Dead Sea
And the dim-glimmering temple.   Then three times
He lifted him aloft to full arm's length,
And danced him up and down delightedly;
Such joy had they that morning on the height,
Such innocent entertainment and such mirth.

CANTO VII.

KING HEROD AND THE YOUNG MOTHER.

UPON a hill which had been formed by art,
By art had been up-piled and sloped, arose
A structure vast and beautiful to view,
Distant from Zion's mount a score of leagues,
Half palace and half fortress.
A town had gathered round the terraced hill,
With circular streets concentric widening out
Into the circumjacent plain afar,
With gardens intermixed and shady groves.
Water on arching aqueducts was borne
From neighboring hills, the purest and the best

To keep the gardens green, the fountains full,
And even to supply with freshening stream
The lofty castle's loftiest marble hall.
Like spokes in some vast wheel, the circular streets
Were cut by others from a central point
Outraying.   This point was the castle's self.
In our own times a city* may be seen
In Germany after this fashion built,
Save that one half consists of mansioned streets,
The other of a park, with avenues
Of shady boscage, spoke-wise, cirque-wise planned,
Each answering to the other.
    The castle, with its appertaining town,
Was named, by him who planned it, from himself,
Herodion.   There the tyrant dwelt, and there
The vision wafts us, showing at a glance
Outside and in, the castle and its lord,
The building and the builder, through and through.
The structure was peculiar.   Lofty stairs,
By more than a hundred steps ascending, led
To a vast, sloping terrace; thence, through gates
Of strongest brass, with bolt and bar made firm,
The way led (woe to most that entered there)
To a broad courtyard, where the measured tread
Of arméd sentinels forever rang
Along the marble pavement day and night.
This passed, a passage long and tortuous, led
Into another court where sentinels
Were also on the watch, forever armed.
In the last courtyard, last and innermost,
Was seen a grim array of instruments
Of torture, of all kinds and every form—
Racks, thumbscrews, pincers (to be used red-hot),

* Carlsruhe, in the Grand Duchy of Baden.

15

The bearer of most glorious news. The Child,
That one day shall be king of all the earth,
As seers foretold and wise men from the east,
And whom you have been searching for in vain,
Has disappeared—the Mother and the Child—
I know where they have fled—the time, the place—
By accident I learned it; no one else
In all Judea knows the secret. Speak
The word, great king, and grant me audience.
I will impart the whole most truthfully,
And spare your majesty a world of toil."
    The king then read the words again—again—
And pondered long upon their import strange.
At last he called for parchment and a pen,
Wrote out a passport to admit the maid,
And sealed it with his royal signet-ring.
    The servant bore it swiftly to the maid,
And bade her follow. Swiftly bolt and bar
Flew backwards; magic-quick then door on door
Flew open; onwards, upwards trod the maid,
With firm, unfaltering footstep. Closely veiled,
She trod before the king and bowed the knee
As if in deep obeisance. Then the king
Gave signal to the servitors to leave
The hall—but with a chosen band—to take
Their stations out of sight, but within call,
Ready to answer any signal-word.
    The servants bowed, obeyed. The hall was left
With only those two human beings in it,
An aged, guilty king—a woman veiled.
    " The writing on this palm-leaf—is it thine ? "
Then asked the wrinkled king, with stealthy glance,
Holding the letter full in sight. " Tis mine."
" Your name ? "   " Salome."   " And your residence ? "

"My home for two years past was Bethlehem,'
Answered the speaker, with a voice so sweet,
So musical, that to his ancient ear
It sounded like the voice of days long past,
When Mariamne lived and called him lord.
"For two most happy years," she spoke again,
"I lived in Bethlehem, in David's town."
"Where were you born?"
                "Upon Judea's hills.
My father was a herdsman, rich in flocks.
I often sported, whilst a child, with lambs,
And early fell in love with innocence.
Five brothers grew up with me; all five strong,
And having in their cheeks the rose of health."
"Have you no sister?"
                "Only one, my lord;
But one most dearly loved."
                "Her name, I pray?"
"Her name? O, how I loved her! Liberty."
  The wrinkled king began to tremble then,
And was about to call aloud for help,
When, lo, as quick as thought, her veil was doffed,
A dagger quivered in her uplift hand,
And, swift as arrow loosened from the bow,
She sprang towards the king, and made a lunge
Directly at his heart. Thanks to his coat of mail—
A miracle of cunning workmanship—
Link upon link and scale on jointed scale—
The dagger glanced aside. The blow had failed.
  The wrinkled king laughed loud with fiendish glee.
"Ha, ha! the surge has tossed against a rock
And broken into foam." Then, stooping down
To seize the dagger fallen from her hand,
And feeling rapidly both edge and point,

"The blow was ably aimed, the weapon keen,"
He said, " pity 't has failed.   In after times
Men would have read how the great Herod fell
Beneath a maiden's arm.   What hinders me
E'en now to sheathe it in thy heart ? "
                                    "My heart
Is ready, eager to receive it.   Strike."
She opened wide her arms, and threw them up,
Expanded wide her chest, like one whose soul
Has lifted her above the fear of death,
Or like some disembodied spirit freed
From flesh, and all its crouching cares and fears,
And which, superior to mortality,
Looks down on kings and boasted kingly power
As something far beneath it.   "Strike, I say;
This heart quails not before King Herod—strike.
I have deceived thee—thus far I've done wrong.
I, who was never known in all my days
To use deceit or falsehood, practiced them
On thee, that I might take away thy life.
Thus much I've erred—may God in heaven forgive me."
She ended with an upward glance, as if
Imploring pardon, not from earthly powers,
But from the great Creator.   As she stood
In this grand attitude, the cruel king,   ·
Wrinkled in front and reprobate at heart,
And clotted o'er and o'er with leprous sin,
E'en he, for one short moment, gazed with awe
And admiration.   In her youthful beauty,
Her symmetry of limb, her faultless form,
He fancied he could see (and so he could)
Some traces of similitude to one
Whom in his noon of manhood he had loved
As much as heart so selfish e'er *could* love—

His murdered Mariamne.   This thought thawed
For one short moment that old Ætna-heart,
Snow-capped and yet volcanic.
                              "Strike, I say,"
She spoke now in a milder, calmer tone,
Like one who, having prophesied the worst,
Looks on the worst with grand tranquillity;
"The world holds now no creature I once loved.
I am no maiden, Herod, but, though young,
I *was* a mother.   Cruel, cruel king!
I had two blooming boys—twins—lovely twins—
So like, their mother scarce knew one from other;
So beautiful, the mountaineers and shepherd-folk
Would flock from miles around to gaze upon them.
Your bloodhounds tracked them out.   They lapped their
      blood.
My husband, noblest, bravest among men,
When he beheld his rosy innocents,
· Dead side by side—stone-dead his darling boys—
Their mother on the ground as if dead too
(I fear he thought I was)—was frenzy-struck,
And as I since have heard, he rushed among
The ruthless soldiers wildly—then with cords
They bound him hand and foot—at night he broke
The ligaments, and wandered off—
No one can tell me where.   I've told my tale."
   Her woman's nature, noble as it was,
Heroic as it had become from woe,
Could stand it now no longer.   In her hands
She hid her lovely face, so finely shaped,
So fashioned by her God to be beloved,
She hid her face and shook.   O, how she sobbed!
That noble, lovely mother, how she sobbed!
And ever as she sobbed, she kept on saying:

"My boys, my boys, my darling twin-born boys."
'Twas well the soldiers waiting near the hall
Had not been present—well for Herod then—
I think they would have torn him limb from limb,
Or hurled him headlong from the balcony.
    She lifted up her head, and dried her tears,
And stood before the tyrant as before,
Defiant and disdainful. Not a worm,
A crawling, slimy, wriggling coffin-worm,
Has e'er excited such a loathing—such
A deep, untold, unwordable disgust,
As did in her that foul, sin-cankered king.
He saw it in her eye, her beautiful face,
Which, like Medusa's (seemed to *him*), though fair,
Fringed round with serpents, each one hissing at him.
His hoary heart 'gan fail. He gave the call,
The signal-call for help. Then arméd men
Rushed in and thronged around. The old king quailed;
But, not to show his fear, he rallied soon,
And bade them for the present stand anear,
But not to offer aught of violence.
The demon in him was again aroused,
The hot, unsating thirst for human blood,
Added to which was hatred of that being
Who looked upon him with such deep disdain.
    Then Herod, for that he was growing weak,
And that his head began to swim, his knees
To knock together, and his jaws to quake,
Between two crouching body-servants, crept
Up to his golden throne, and took his seat,
Pale, haggard, and bewildered. Then he called
For wine to give him strength—wine came—he drank.
This turned his weakness to convulsive force,
To fearful wreathing spasms. The pains of hell

Seemed to torment him ere his time; hell-fire
(In latent, inward shape, but true hell-fire)
Seemed creeping serpentlike through all his limbs,
Through all his vital parts, with withering heat.
For years those symptoms had been coming on,
Nor was the spectacle, so dread to see,
New to the guards or courtiers.
                              When the fit
Had spent its force, he looked around the hall,
, And saw Sàlome standing, statue-like,
In all the beauty of young womanhood,
Collected, self-contained, as if nor guards
Nor courtiers, servants, king nor kingly hall
Concerned her aught.
                    Then spoke the king again,
As soon as he had rallied from the fit,
And said: "Salome, listen. Thou hast tried
With sacrilegious hand to kill thy king.
For this the punishment by law is death.
But simple death is punishment too slight.
In thy case, torture must precede thy death.
Thou hast beheld my implements below,
How cunningly devised they are; how fit
To answer the great purpose they subserve.
Salome, take thy choice. The cross, the rack,
The dropping grate (the same great Solomon
Used in Gehenna, when the children's cries
Were smothered in the din of drums and cymbals,
Whilst sacrificed to Moloch), the spiked tun
(Like that in which great Regulus once rolled),
The brazen bull, modeled from that which bears
The name of old Phaláris— these thou'st seen,
And more beside. Salome, take thy choice."
    "Tyrant, I'll make no choice," Salome said,

"As sure as God's above, and thou sit'st there
On yonder golden throne the food for worms,
Before thy sepulcher is closed above thee,
Salome ne'er shall be thy tortured victim.
I know my Maker would not suffer it.
Before the screws were squeezed, the rack were stretched,
The grate were heated, or the spiked tun rolled,
An angel's wing, commissioned from above,
Would bear me from thy power.   I fear thee not."
　　Then spoke the king again, with mocking calm:
"Or wouldst thou rather, my Salome dear,
Tread downwards to that subterranean realm
Which reaches far beneath this castle?   Ha!
Deep, darksome dens are there, unwholesome, damp,
Where the toad houses, and the coiling snake,
Where not one ray of sunlight ever came,
Where e'en the spider can not live and spin,
Where never any sounds but groans were heard,
Or clank of eating chains.   Come, take thy choice."
　　Then spoke Salome, with a calm, firm voice:
"Thy dungeons I fear not.   Not mine to tread
Adown the steps that lead to that dread realm.
Salome has lived free—free shall she die—
Free as when erst my native mountain breeze
Freshened this youthful cheek.   I fear thee not."
　　"Now, soldiers, seize her," thundered forth the king.
The dagger which the king had clutched—and dropped—
Salome's dagger, still lay there concealed
In shadow on the floor.   Like lightning-flash,
Salome leaped and seized it.   Equal speed
Drove on her hand—her arm.   The dagger flashed
One instant in her grasp—the next it tapped
Her life-blood.   How it streamed—that noble blood!
Then, staggering forwards a few steps, she flung

The dagger at the panic-stricken king,
And stained his royal robe. "Free, free," she cried,
"Salome's spirit rises free to heaven,
Whilst thou, a crawling reptile, slim'st the clod,
Sin-spotted, ripe for hell."
                            Then down she sank,
As though life's hour-glass sands were nearly spent.
Once only did she rise upon one arm,
And, opening wide her eyes, like one who scans
The future, seer-like, and in words distinct,
But somewhat disarranged, and frequent pause,
She cried: "I see a star—God's Morning Star—
How bright! how bright! Before creation's dawn
Shone forth—*that* shone. Clear day will follow soon.
The Holy Babe is safe—the tyrant foiled—
Oh, glory, glory to the Lord of Hosts—
Night flies—Oh—I can say no more—my breath—
Is spent. Night flies—day overfloods the world—
Hail, holy Light Divine!—All hail—all hail."
These were the last words fair Salome spoke.
Even Death stole not all beauty from the face,
For there the body lay as in a trance,
With gently smiling lips and open eyes,
As though they saw far off a full-sphered light
Rising above the nations. Joy, O, joy!

NOTES.

PAGE 35, CANTO I.

Cavern's Mouth.—For an excellent account of these curiously excavated caverns in the neighborhood of Hebron, I would refer the reader to Thompson's "The Land and the Book;" as also to Robinson's Book of Travel through Palestine.· They were formed in the soft limestone, or chalky rock, which abounds in that part of Judea. Low, arched passages were cut in the rock, leading into larger excavations. Some of these last consisted of domes or bell-shaped apartments, from twenty to thirty feet high from the floor, and in diameter from twelve to twenty feet. The top of the dome has usually a small circular opening at the surface of the ground above, admitting light into the cavern. For the most part there were three or four of these chambers together, communicating with each other. The miraculous light, referred to in the poem, is supposed to issue through the circular opening alluded to, and may be imagined to spread towards heaven in the form of an inverted cone.

PAGE 100, CANTO IX.

THE ANOINTED DOVE.

"The attractive power of sweet ointments, to which Solomon here alludes, is notably declared in that which Basil relates of the manner of catching doves; which was by breeding one up tame, and then anointing her wings, they let her fly away, and the sweet odor of the ointment drew abundance of pigeons after · her, which she brought to the cot of her owner."—*Patrick's Commentary on the Song of Solomon.*

'Midst rocks and caverns, all alone,
A white-winged dove was heard to moan;
All day, all night, forlorn she sate,
Without a friend, without a mate.

One morn a holy man passed by,
With snowy beard and prayerful eye;
A censer on his arm he swings,
With which he fumes the sad bird's wings.

Charmed by the force of odors bland,
The lone one perches on his hand;
And then, with liquids heavenly sweet,
He bathes her eyes, her plumes, her feet.

All dripping thus with holy dew,
As up morn's roseate clouds she flew,
Of God's own garden the perfume
Streamed on her track from every plume.

For leagues on leagues those sweets she fanned
O'er winding stream and desert sand.
And crowded caravans, 'tis said,
With all the camels, knelt and prayed.

"Is Eden floating down, indeed?"
The Arab cried, and reined his steed:
"Or hover o'er yon groves of palm
Sweet angels, veiled in clouds of balm?"

Meanwhile, amidst those caverns rude,
All day the holy hermit stood,
Oft gazing eastward in the air,
As if winged visitors were there.

Clambering at eve a lofty rock,
He saw a rainbow-tinted flock
Of doves fly towards the sinking sun;
All circling round th' Anointed One.

"O Innocence!" the old man cried,
"Thou comest back, a spotless bride;
Where'er thy heaven-sweet wings are found,
The sister virtues flock around."

ERRATA.

———'

Page 8, line 19; for Arno, read Anio.

Page 15, line 24; for words, read worlds.

Page 20, line 19; for Madagascar's isle, read Ceylon's torrid isle.

Page 21, first note; the note should read: For some account of this curious phenomenon, see Ansichten von der Nachtseite der Naturwissenschaft, von Dr. Gotthilf Heinrich von Schubert.

Page 27, line 19; for brines, read brine.

www.ingramcontent.com/pod-product-compliance
Lightning Source LLC
Chambersburg PA
CBHW030121030726
47498CB00007B/2489